Donna and the Fatman

Helen Zahavi was born in London, and worked as a Russian translator before becoming a writer. Her first novel, *Dirty Weekend*, has been translated into thirteen languages and was made into a film. Three years ago she moved to Paris, where she discovered calvados and wrote *Donna and the Fatman*.

Praise for *Dirty Weekend*:

'From the opening lines the repetitive, hypnotic authority of the prose takes over . . . as a piece of stylised thuggery – mordant humour run riot – the effect is stunning'

SARAH EDWORTHY, *MARIE CLAIRE*

'A stripped down Martin Amis . . . its rhythms are so insistent as to be metrical: entire paragraphs could be relineated as verse. The dialogue inclines to Pinteresque . . . the novel will be seen as a companion piece to Elizabeth Smart's *By Grand Central Station*'

MARTIN CROPPER, *SUNDAY TELEGRAPH*

Praise for *True Romance*:

'She is witty and knowing and she manipulates words with real genius . . . Zahavi and Jeanette Winterson are among the best young writers around today'

CARMEN CALLIL, *DAILY TELEGRAPH*

By the same author

DIRTY WEEKEND
TRUE ROMANCE

DONNA AND THE FATMAN

Helen Zahavi

TRANSWORLD PUBLISHERS LTD
61–63 Uxbridge Road, London W5 5SA

TRANSWORLD PUBLISHERS (AUSTRALIA) PTY LTD
15–20 Helles Avenue, Moorebank, NSW 2170

TRANSWORLD PUBLISHERS (NZ) LTD
3 William Pickering Drive, Albany, Auckland

Published by Anchor – a division of Transworld Publishers Ltd

First published in Great Britain by Anchor, 1998

Copyright © 1998 Helen Zahavi

The right of Helen Zahavi to be identified as the author of this work has been asserted in accordance with the Copyright, Designs and Patents Act 1988

A catalogue record for this book is available from the British Library

ISBN 1862 30045 3

All rights reserved. No part of this publication may be reproduced, stored in a retrieval system, or transmitted in any form or by any means, electronic, mechanical, photocopying, recording, or otherwise, without the prior permission of the publishers

Typeset in 11/14pt Adobe Caslon by Phoenix Typesetting, West Yorkshire
Printed in Great Britain by Mackays of Chatham plc, Chatham, Kent

for Miriam and Alter

1

A mile or so from Hackney, more or less in Dalston, is a pasta place the locals know as Carlo's. It's buried down the end of a cul-de-sac and it can take a while to find it, but it's a laid-back kind of place, all golden light and mellow wood, the sort of place that beckons you in on a wet November evening.

So when two young men came through the door – a skinhead one and a normal one – no-one really looked at them. About a dozen people having a feed, and no-one really stared at them. Well-built men with perfect teeth, they smiled a lot, and who could blame them.

'You hungry, Merv?'

'Bit peckish, frankly.'

'Get a menu, shall I?'

'If you wouldn't mind.'

The skinhead one, who had a shiny scalp, began moving

round the room. He threaded his way between the tables and watched the punters tucking in. Now and then he passed a remark, if he thought it might be helpful – asked them if they liked his hair, or told them food was good for them – but he mostly merely stood and watched.

'Don't mind me,' he'd say. 'I'm only looking.'

And when they heard that slightly lisping voice and saw the polished ankle-boots they'd suddenly lose their appetite, at which he'd throb and glow with pleasure, he'd almost spurt with satisfaction. For he liked himself, immensely. He was a fine young man, in his opinion. He was benevolence personified. A decent bloke with a shaven skull. He might have scratched too much, but he couldn't help it, for he always itched when he interacted. He often rubbed himself when he made new friends.

But he had this need for conversation, and when he saw the couple by the window, oblivious and self-absorbed, they seemed so clean and virtuous, such pure and wholesome citizens, that he thought he'd introduce himself, he felt he'd better say hello.

'That looks tasty.'

He bent and peered.

'It got a name?'

The husband studied the razored scalp.

'Zabaglione.'

The skinhead frowned.

'Not English, then.'

'Not really.'

'Nice, though, is it?'

'It's one of our favourites.' A nervous cough. 'We always have it.'

'For your afters . . .'

'You should try it, sometime.'

The skinhead nodded.

'Well just a weeny bit, as you're offering,' and he dipped his finger into the bowl, scooped out some stuff, and licked it off. A moment's contemplation, as he thought the matter over, and then he said:

'Bit sweet, old mate, if I'm being honest.'

He turned to the wife.

'You come here often?'

And while she's fumbling for an answer, he hears footsteps behind and his master's voice:

'Billy.'

'Merv . . . ?'

'The kitchen.'

'Right.'

He bowed politely to the lady, and followed his friend into heat and steam. There were two men in there and they didn't look well. They had a nervous look, if you really looked. The chef was standing by the knife-rack. Didn't pick one up, but he stayed close by. The other man was slightly older, tinted glasses and manicured nails. About forty-five, if you felt like counting. A well-pressed suit and slicked-back hair and sweating, fairly heavily.

The one called Mervyn smiled at him.

'Hello, Carlo. All right, are we?'

The kitchen so hot it was like a sauna. He unbuttoned his jacket.

'Where's the waiter?'

'He went out the back. Took the service exit.'

'Wise lad, I reckon. Pissed off back to Naples, he's any sense. And who can blame him, all these rowdy East End types.'

'He comes from Wembley.'

'Someone has to.'

There was hardly room to move in there, not with four of

them, not crammed in tight. Mervyn licked his lips. The air felt moist, as though sticking to his skin. He gazed at the cook, quietly weighed him up.

'I think it's time you went,' he said.

He stepped towards him, right up close. They were nearly touching, almost kissing.

'We've come for a chat with the boss-man, see? Got to talk to Mister Carlo.'

He plucked a jacket off a hook. Shoved it against the man's chest.

'So fuck off home, you're breathing my air.'

The man didn't move. He was a wiry man, used to chopping things up. A faint, pink flush spread over his neck. Pin-drop silence. He stared at the boys. You listened hard, you heard adrenalin pumping. Ten long seconds of exquisite tension, and Carlo touched his arm, murmured something. The man seemed to hesitate, then shrugged and left. They watched the door bang shut behind him, heard the footsteps getting quieter.

Billy sighed, a soft and wistful exhalation.

'Pity, that.'

He scratched his cheek.

'Almost had a scene there, Merv, and I like a scene.'

'I know you do.'

Mervyn checked his watch. Nearly half eleven. He glanced at the owner.

'You got it ready?'

'You need to ask?'

'So you've got it, right?'

Carlo nodded glumly. He took out an envelope and passed it over.

'I can't do this, Mervyn.'

'You can if you try.'

'I'm bleeding, see.'

Mervyn weighed the envelope in his hand. It felt pleasantly thick.

'You got a problem?'

'I'm only saying.'

'Well say it to the big man, cause he'll be here soon.'

The skinhead leaned forward.

'He coming round tonight, then?'

'I think so, Billy. He'll be dropping by.'

Mervyn pushed past him and opened the door.

'He gets these whims,' he murmured. 'Likes to keep his hand in.'

He led them back into the dining room. It was virtually empty, almost devoid of customers. They'd abandoned half-eaten dinners, and barely-touched desserts, and picked up their coats and departed. An all but vacant restaurant. Very nearly no-one there. Just some girl, some bit of nothing, sitting in the corner.

Billy stared round the room and scraped his neck. He dug in his nails where it always itched.

'Where's the punters, Merv?'

'All gone, Billy.'

The skinhead looked a touch perturbed.

'Was it something I said?'

Mervyn straightened his tie.

'Might have been.' He checked his cuffs. 'You never know.'

He walked over to the girl and pulled out a chair.

'Hello, darling. You still here?'

She flicked her eyes towards him. The red mouth opened.

'Apparently.'

'Apparently,' he repeated softly. 'You're apparently still here. But the thing is, see, the question truly is, my love: *why* are you still here?'

He sat down and took out his fags and looked her over. Not

bad, he thought. Bit scruffy, maybe, but he wouldn't say no. She'd do for a night out in Dalston. He shook one clear of the pack and she pulled it slowly out and slid it between her lips. Short, black skirt, and looking at him in that certain way. He struck a match and leaned towards her.

'You miss your bus, or something?'

She sucked in tar and nicotine, then blew out smoke in a thin, grey plume.

'I'm waiting for my coffee.'

He stuck the burnt match in the corner of his mouth. She had her charms, he told himself. Not too many, but one or two. The scarlet nails, the lippiness, that pure, perverted skirt.

'Hear that, Carlo? Let's have some liquid for the lady.'

She flicked off ash and studied him, took in the dove-grey suit and the well-cut hair.

'I didn't catch your name.'

'I'm Mervyn, sweetheart. Known as Merv the Perv.'

She watched him lean back in the chair. A big, young lad. Lot of attitude.

'That your car outside?'

'You want a ride?'

'Because I quite like Jags.'

'It's a Daimler, actually.'

'Posh sort of car for such a rough sort of bloke.'

She glanced at his shoes. They were quality shoes.

'You make a living, do you?'

'I get by, I guess.'

'Doing what, exactly?'

He gazed at her and clicked his knuckles.

'People give me money.'

She moved the ashtray nearer.

'That's kind of them.'

'I know it is. They've got generous natures.'

'That why they do it?'

'Perhaps they like me.'

'Why else, Merv?'

'Why else what?'

'Why else do they give you all that dough?'

He flipped the matchstick across his mouth.

''Cause I'm a thug, darling.'

He spread his legs and smiled.

'I'm a nasty piece of work.'

She was still digesting this useful news when there was a tinkling sound, and the skinhead approached with a plastic tray. Shuffling slowly, an ape with an orchid. He put it down and laid out cups and saucers. Mervyn swivelled his head.

'You joining us, are you? That's always a pleasure, son. Always delightful. Now pour it out, why don't you.'

Billy nodded across the table.

'Who's this, then?'

'It's a girl, Billy. *You* remember: curves and stuff. Monthly emanations.'

He watched the skinhead start to pour.

'You want to try it, sometime.'

'Who says I haven't?'

'I know you haven't.'

'You know that, do you?'

''Case you get germs.'

'I'm careful, that's all.'

'You're a fucking monk.'

'It's a free country, right?'

'So it's free,' Merv said. 'So what?'

'So no-one has to, unless they want to.'

'Thing is, Billy, you're meant to want to.'

'Oh yeah? Says who?'

Mervyn shook his head.

'I can't talk to you, can I?'

Billy spooned three sugars into his cup.

'Well fucking fuck off, then. Right?'

'Yeah, right.'

Mervyn grinned and sipped his coffee, and they sat there, quietly bonding, the loving little threesome. For a few brief minutes, no-one spoke. Carlo hovered near the bar, and the clock on the wall showed ten to twelve, and the light was low, and the jazz was soft, and it's a mile or so from Hackney, more or less in Dalston, the sort of place that beckons you in on a wet November evening.

Billy drained his cup and placed it carefully on the saucer. He liked things neat and tidy, bit of order in his life. He fixed her with his skinhead stare.

'You staying round here?'

'For a day or two.'

'Thought you might be. I thought to myself, she looks the type who's passing through. That's what I thought, see, when I saw you. That you look like someone . . . transient.'

Peering closer, like she's zabaglione.

'Not whiffsome, exactly, but not very kempt.'

A thoughtful scratch of flaking cheek.

'Some kind of vagrant, are you?'

'Something like that.'

He hooked his thumbs around his braces and leaned back in the chair.

'Need money, right?'

'Might do.'

'Cause we can smell it, see, that needy smell.'

He glanced at the window and cocked his head. A car was pulling up outside, the well-tuned engine quietly purring. That muted sound of wealth and steel.

'Should we help her, Merv?'

'Fair question, Billy.'

They pondered a while, then Mervyn said:

'Would a tenner, do?'

The skinhead reflected. He was thinking it over.

'Ten, you said.'

'Maybe eleven.'

'As a gift, you mean?'

'More like a fee,' Merv said.

He gazed at her. He was feeling good. Feeling like a young thug should.

'A tenner, darling. What do you say?'

He pulled open his tie.

'Nice and friendly, nothing nasty.'

Car doors slamming.

'Perhaps over the table, as it's handy. No point shooting home, cause I've never been one for sheets and pillows. Bit poncey, really, if I'm being honest.'

Footsteps on the pavement.

'Just let him clear away the cups, OK? Cause I'm not too keen on dirty cups. So what d'you reckon? Be a bargain, really: couple of minutes, the old in-out, and there's ten in your hand and off you go.'

The hairless chin. The rinsed-out eyes.

'Can't give you more, sugar, as times are hard, but it's the thought that counts, I've always said. Billy won't mind. That right, Billy?'

'Feel free, my son. You do your stuff.'

'Hear that, did you? Billy says fine, so we'll just have a quickie. Being as it's Sunday, and as you're passing through.'

He leaned towards her. The urgent Mervyn hiss.

'So how about it, sweetheart?'

At which propitious moment, the street door was shoved open and a gust of cold air swept across the floor and came licking round her ankles. She glanced over. A dark-haired guy in a black leather jacket was standing just inside, and a vague, unsettling recognition began growing in her brain: He's mine, she realized. The one for me. And suddenly, as if from nowhere:

'Move it, Joe. You're blocking my way.'

A mammoth form, a mound of pink and shining flesh, had rolled benignly through the door. Sixteen stone of fat and gristle, and a shock of carrot hair. Breasts, she thought. He's got generous breasts. She stared at him, tried to guess his age. Maybe sixty, give or take, which is almost dead to a girl like her. Almost buried, the way she saw it. But even so, a man who mattered, a man who had significance. You could sense the tension breaking out, the air become electric. He unbuttoned his coat and approached the table.

'Shift yourself, Billy. There's a good lad.'

The skinhead got up and the big man sat down. He flicked some breadcrumbs to the floor.

'Evening, boys.'

Cigar-stub clamped between his teeth. A confident man, the way he acted. Would have a bob or two, which always helped. Mervyn took the envelope out of his pocket and placed it on the table. The fat man laid his hand on top, as if making a benediction, as if communing with his private god.

'All been counted?'

Mervyn nodded, and the man slipped the envelope inside his coat. His eyes went flicking round the table.

'Everything all right, then?'

'More or less,' Mervyn said. 'Carlo's upset.'

'That a fact?'

The man half-turned so he was facing the bar.

'You not happy, son?'

The owner shrugged.

'Come on, Carlo, don't be shy.'

'I got business problems. Too many overheads.'

'You ought to sack the waiter, I mean he's bone fucking idle.'

Carlo tried to smile. Managed a baring of the teeth.

'I went round the doctor. Got some pills.'

The big man shifted on his seat.

'You want to stay away from pills, you mark my words. They're garbage, see? Full of shit and chemicals. Very bad news are pills, old mate.'

'But I got worries, Henry.'

'We've all got *them*, pal. So what are yours?'

'This place, isn't it. I mean half the profit getting skimmed, so I feel like I'm working for nothing, see.'

Henry shook his head.

'I take your point, believe me. But you know what they say, right? Neither a borrower nor a lender be.'

A sympathetic shrug.

'Specially not a borrower.'

Carlo stared at the floor.

'I could give up the business.'

'You most certainly could.' The sound as he sucked on a hand-rolled cigar. 'But the debt, like the struggle, continues.'

'I'm getting stress here, Henry. You know what I'm saying?'

The fat man sighed.

'That's because you work too hard. Because you don't know how to delegate. You want to be like me, see? Be more relaxed, try and take things easy. You want some good advice? Close up tomorrow, motor down to Sussex for the day. Have a holiday, old son, cause you deserve it. Get away from all the riff-raff, breathe some decent English air. I mean it can't be bad, can it?'

He turned back to the table.

'It's OK,' he announced. 'He's happy now.'

He slid the sugar-bowl away from him. There were brown

smears inside where one of the boys had dipped in a wet spoon, and he'd always found such things distressing.

He glanced at Mervyn.

'So here we are, then,' he murmured. 'Right, Merv?'

'Right.'

Henry squinted at the girl.

'She's looking bored.'

'Boss?'

'Your lady friend.'

'She was waiting for her coffee.'

'Well she's had it now.'

'You want her to leave?' Mervyn, ever helpful. 'Want her chucked outside?'

'Manners, Merv.'

The big boss smiled, showing neat yellow dentures. He held out his hand.

'Henry,' he announced, and squeezed her palm. 'They call me the fatman, but I don't mind.'

'Donna,' she said.

The skinhead sniggered.

'Donna Kebab.'

The fatman pointed at the boy in leather, who'd pulled up a chair and flipped it round, and now sat quietly straddling it, all bulging crotch and faded denim.

'That one's Joe, as you're asking. My boy,' he said, 'my Joey-boy.'

He leaned across and cuffed him lightly on the head. Joey-boy, with his pale blue eyes and his near-black hair. Looked like such a wild young man. You looked at Joe, and you wouldn't know that he lived in a basement flat, and slept in a single bed, and ate from tins and paper bags, and held his essence in his hands, and loathed himself with the pure and utter certainty of one who knows he can't be wrong. But he looked like such a wild young man.

'He's everything to me. That right, lads? My driver, gofer, faithful friend. He's the baseline, the constant point of reference, my poor but honest Joey-boy. He's where I started from, and I keep him by my side to measure just how far I've come.'

The flesh of his neck seemed to quiver slightly when he turned his head, as though it were almost liquid, as though you could almost spoon it up and have it for dessert.

'Will you look at her watching, eh? Giving us the eyeball. Like she thinks she'll sum us up. You've told her all our little secrets, have you? Filled the girly in? Because she's looking pretty eager, frankly, looking pretty hopeful. So what I'm wondering, see, is does she know we're bad boys? Think she knows that? Eh, Joe? Eh?'

He leaned his bulk towards her, and she was suddenly aware of a milky smell, an infant scent surrounding him that made her think of baby food and nappies.

'D'you know that, sweetheart? They tell you, did they?'

The pale, grey tongue between his lips. The odour of milk and drooping age.

'Speak to me, darling. Just open your mouth.'

She slowly uncrossed and recrossed her legs, taking her time, for she's in no great rush. A single, fluid movement in black, velvet skirt and sling-back shoes. She stubbed out her fag and looked at him. For the very first time since he'd come inside, she took a good look at the fatman.

'Hello, Henry.'

'Hello, sugar.'

'You saying you're bad?'

You could see him relax, you could feel him unwind.

'I'm fucking evil.'

'What's your line, then?'

'Have a guess.'

'You're sort of in business.'

'Well put there, darling, because sort of in business is what I am.'

'What kind of thing, exactly?'

'Little bit of this,' he said. 'Little bit of that.'

He removed the cigar-butt from his mouth and rolled it between his fingers.

'Let's just say that I'm involved in various enterprises, I have my finger in various pies, I've pushed my thumb in a number of rectums.'

He paused to search for the perfect phrase.

'Venture capital, kind of thing.'

'Like a bank,' she suggested.

'That's right, sweetheart. I lend people money, then I ask for it back.'

She plucked a speck of cotton from her sleeve.

'Is that called financial services?'

'No, darling.'

He shoved the cigar-stub back in his mouth.

'It's called demanding money with menaces.'

He bent towards her. The small, wet mouth beside her ear.

'I don't need the money,' he confided. 'I do it for the menaces.'

The milky breath in her face.

'You were telling us about your bloke, I think.'

'Haven't got a bloke.'

'But you've had a bloke.'

'One or two.'

'Tell me about the last one,' he said. 'Tell me about the last one who touched you where you're tender.'

The plump, warm hand that brushed her thigh.

'Was he like Merv, or was he like me?'

She shifted her weight on the seat, moved fractionally away from him.

'Afraid I've got to go now, Henry. Another time, perhaps.' Apologetic shrug. 'It's been nice, though . . .'

'Hasn't it.'

He sighed his fatman sigh and leaned back in the chair, spreading slightly over the edges, oozing contentment from his open pores. A profoundly happy man.

'So you're off, then, are you?'

He watched her bend and pick up her bag.

'Got a nice flat?'

'Might have.'

'That's grand,' he said. 'I'm glad you've got a home,' he said, 'because some people haven't, see. I mean dosser-type people. You seen them, right? Spit a lot, because they've got TB. Crap on the pavement and ask you for money. Ought to lock them up, you with me, Merv? Cause they're a blight on the city.'

'They're a fucking disgrace.'

'But you got a home, sugar, and you're laughing. You got a room, you got no problem.'

The piggy eyes were focused on her face.

'And if you haven't, we can fix you up. Just ask us nicely and we'll sort something out.'

He passed a hand across his scalp. Smoothing down the dry, red hair.

'So which one you want, then, the boss or a lackey?'

A millisecond's hesitation, and she flicked a glance at the leather-boy. Mervyn grunted, Billy sighed. There was a ripple of disappointment, a collective recognition of pleasure postponed.

Henry smiled thinly.

'I know that look,' he said. 'I think she likes you, Joey. You're well away there, son. Got your entrance ticket for that one, if I'm not being too crude, as I sometimes am.'

A sudden frown.

'Excuse me, ladies.'

He hawked up phlegm and spat it smoothly into a pale blue handkerchief.

'That's better,' he grunted. 'Clear out the old lungs.'

He allowed himself a brief, admiring glance at the glob of creamy sputum, then shoved the hankie back in his pocket. He put his hand on Joe's shoulder and heaved himself up.

'Be needing you in the morning,' he said. 'Come round at ten.'

'I'm down the gym.'

'You some kind of nancy, now? Stuff the gym, son. Just be on time.'

He buttoned up his coat.

'If you're still on speakers, you can bring her with.'

He motioned Merv and Billy to follow, then took her hand, brushed it with his lips.

'You made the right choice, believe me. Picked a winner, frankly. Got some style, my Joey-boy. Knows how to treat the ladies. Always splashing out, he is: a burger here, a milk shake there. You be a good girl, you'll get porridge for brekker.'

'I quite like porridge.'

'Thought you might.'

He was squeezing her fingers, holding them tight.

'So time to say goodnight, then, is it?'

'It's been a pleasure, Henry.'

'More than that, darling. It's been delightful.' A joyless smile. 'Until tomorrow, then.'

She eased her hand away.

'Keep well,' she urged. 'And look after those lungs.'

'I'll do my best.'

His bleak, unblinking eyes.
'Sweet dreams, sweetheart.'
She patted his arm.
'And you, Henry.'

2

She woke up in an unfamiliar bed. An acid, grey light was seeping through the curtain and the air smelled damp. She rubbed her eyes and stared at the ceiling. Her bones felt stiff. A rasping noise, a kind of rhythmic grating, seemed to fill the room, a familiar, early-morning sound which she couldn't quite identify. She rolled on to her elbow and saw Joey standing by the sink, scraping black bits off burnt toast. It's an encouraging sign for girls like her, because they like a man who's good in the kitchen, they like them when they're handy.

'Sleep well, did you . . . ?'

He had his back to her, was speaking over his shoulder. Looking good, she thought. Stonewashed jeans and crew-neck vest, and he was looking pretty good.

'Not very. How about you?'

'I was on the floor, wasn't I. Bad for my back.'

She allowed herself a sympathetic yawn.

'But good for your character.'

He dropped some crusts into the pedal bin.

'Only I was wondering, see, cause you were making these sounds all night.'

She frowned at the pillow.

'What sounds?'

'You know.' He shrugged. 'Sort of . . . air sounds.'

'Oh.'

She let this filter through her skull and settle in her brain.

'You saying I snore?'

'Not as such.' His neck went pink. 'Not exactly.'

'That's all right, then, cause if we're being personal, here . . .'

'I know, OK?'

'I mean, that bog you've got . . .'

'I *know*, all right?'

He came back out holding two large plates heaped with charred and cooling pieces of bread.

'Want to clean it, do you?'

The clear blue eyes and the broad Joey grin. He's mine, she thought. He's the one for me.

'Think I'll pass,' she said.

A flat and muscular stomach, like the ones you see in magazines, and he hadn't shaved, which always helped. Could do a lot worse, she told herself.

'Because I'm not too partial to chores and things. Domestic stuff . . .' she pulled a face, '. . . not really *me*.'

'But you could try,' he persisted.

'I could,' she agreed. 'But I think I won't.'

He put the plates on the table and pulled up a chair.

'You having some, are you, or you just want to watch?'

'Depends what you've got. Cause I'm picky, Joey. I've been indulged.'

'There's strawberry jam, cheese slices, a bit of marge . . .'

She rolled out of bed.

'Butter me some toast, then, Joe.'

She wandered over to the table.

'Not too much,' she added, 'just a scraping.'

She sat down opposite him. They smiled at each other, for it would happen soon. He dug his knife into the plastic tub.

'Cheese or jam?'

'Both, I reckon.'

'You can't have both.'

He draped a slice of processed cheese onto a piece of toast and passed it across.

'I'm the guest, Joe,' she pointed out.

She placed a spoonful of jam on top of the cheese, and smeared it all over with her thumb.

'I can have what I like.'

And having thus laid down the rules of their relationship, breakfast was duly consumed.

They left the flat around nine-thirty, Joe allowing a good half-hour to get from Kilburn up to Hampstead in the fag-end of the rush-hour. A touch cautious, she felt, as they cruised up Carlton Vale. A shade anal, perhaps, though she didn't want to mention it. The car was a late-model BMW, an executive motor with soft leather seats. It was the third-favourite in Henry's collection, he told her, the first being his Bentley and the second his Mercedes Sports.

'What about Mervyn's Jag?'

'You mean his Daimler?'

'Yeah.'

'That's Henry's, too.'

She stared out of the window.

'So everything's Henry's.'

Joe changed up to third.

'More or less.'

They crawled along West End Lane and took a right up Lymington Road. He had one hand on the wheel, the other resting on his thigh. Now and then, she felt him glance across, as if to check she was really there, as if he couldn't quite believe she was almost his, she was very nearly Joey's girl. He cut across the junction, put his foot down hard, and they were climbing the slope of Arkwright Road. The German engine barely murmured. She loved that car, really loved that car. Bit of quality in a tacky world. Should be his, she thought. Not right that Joe had nothing.

When they turned into Fitzjohn's Avenue, the traffic was barely moving. The fumes were already building up, the air was beginning to thicken. But Hampstead Village, all the same, so you had to make allowances. He flipped the gear-stick into second.

'Like to live here, would you?'

She checked her lipstick.

'Might consider it.'

He took a left into Church Row, went twenty yards up Frognal, then left again into Redington Road. He parked about halfway down and pulled on the handbrake. She gazed at the houses. Unattainable houses.

'We double back or something?'

Joe switched off the engine.

'Thought we'd take the scenic route.'

She pulled on her calfskin gloves. The one good thing that she had to her name, a pair of calfskin gloves.

'Can I ask you something?'

'Course you can.'

'How does he manage to fit in the Merc?'

Joe thought it over.

'We lever him in, then we spoon him out.'

It was eight minutes to ten. Henry emerged at three minutes past. He walked up the short drive and climbed carefully inside, easing his soft bulk into the back seat. The car was suddenly filled with a faint, almost imperceptible, odour. It floated quietly in the air and swirled around her head.

'Hope you had a pleasant night,' he said. 'Hope my boy was gentle.'

He flicked the back of his hand against Joe's head. He sort of slapped him, sort of gently.

'That right, son?'

Another smack, slightly harder.

'You been tender with the lady?'

The car dipped as he leaned forward. His mouth was open, and that whiff again, that old man's breath.

'He behave, did he? You can tell *me*, sweetheart, cause we're all friends here. Just say it, sugar, just spit it out. Cause I like my boys to toe the line, so tell me, darling, cause I need to know.'

That Henry smell, blowing in her face.

'Boiled milk,' she muttered.

'What's that, sweetheart?'

'He didn't do anything, Henry.'

'You sure about that?'

'I think I would have noticed.'

'Maybe when you weren't looking . . .'

'Doubt it.'

'While you were sleeping . . .'

'Couldn't sleep, Henry. Not on that bed.'

The fatman snorted.

'What d'you expect? Cause that's a poor man's bed, see. That's the bed you get when you choose the driver not the boss.'

Joe turned the key in the ignition. The engine fired. He glanced into the rear-view mirror.

'Where to?'

A neutral voice. You couldn't gauge him by his voice.

'You asking, Joe?'

'I'm asking.'

The fatman leaned back in the seat. He settled himself down, made himself comfortable.

'Have to think about that,' he murmured. 'Got to have a little ponder.'

He took out a small cigar and slowly unpeeled the cellophane. Where to? he wondered. It was an interesting question, almost metaphysical. Whose life should he enhance today? To which unpaid debt should he attend? Which part of town should he deign to grace with his splendid fatman presence? He quietly mulled it over. He indulged in rumination.

'You know something,' he said finally, popping the cigarillo into his mouth, 'it's such a pleasant day, and I'm feeling so at peace with life, that I think I'd like to visit Trevor.'

3

He placed a black-gloved finger on the buzzer and pressed twice. Cleared his throat and waited.

'I'd like you to meet some friends of mine.'

Monday morning in Acton Town, and a sour, November wind came whipping down the street, bringing fumes and filth from Hanger Lane.

'They have to live above the shop, poor bastards.'

She stared at the window display. Cheap gold bracelets arrayed on fake blue velvet. Low-grade stuff, for girls like her.

'Decent folk,' he added. 'You know the sort.'

He was standing beside her, pressed up close. A different coat from yesterday's. Camel-hair this time, which didn't suit him. Her head felt raw from lack of sleep. She glanced over her shoulder. Joe was waiting in the car, fifty yards back down the traffic-clogged road. Nowhere to park these days, Henry had said. Almost no point having a motor, he'd said. Almost worth it taking the Tube, he'd said, if you didn't mind humanity, if you weren't averse to body smells. She shivered inside her jacket, felt him slip an arm around her shoulder.

'You ought to eat more,' he murmured. 'Get something hot inside you, of a morning.'

Smiling at her with his soft, pink lips.

'Do you like nice things?'

He had an unexpected voice. Never strident, never rasping. A fairly classless, vaguely London, voice. You couldn't place him from the way he spoke, couldn't size him up and pin him down, establish where he came from. And quietly, almost in a whisper. You had to listen closely to the words. You had to cock an ear, and hold your breath, and strain to catch the whispered words of Henry.

The arm around her shoulders, the silent squeeze of ownership.

'Cause if you like nice things, be nice to me.'

He put his finger on the button, and this time held it down until a man appeared inside, a thin-faced, dark-suited man who hurried to the door. They watched him fumble for the keys, and then locks were turned, bolts pulled back, and the plate-glass door swung open.

A moment's pause, then:

'Hello, Trevor. Me again.'

He took her by the elbow and they stepped inside. Warmth, she thought, approvingly. The fatman cast a critical look around.

'Bit dark in here,' he observed. 'Bit gloomy.'

He strode into the middle of the shop.

'Let's have some light, then. There's a good lad.'

The jeweller mumbled his excuses and flicked a switch. Light flooded down.

'I almost thought you weren't in,' Henry said. 'I almost did.'

'My wife was sleeping,' the man said. 'Didn't want to disturb her,' he said, 'not this early in the morning. All that buzzing...' he added. 'I'm afraid you woke her up.'

Henry nodded. The bleak, unblinking eyes.

'Don't be afraid.'

'She's not well, Henry.'

'And I'm sorry to hear it, believe me. Most distressed, in fact. Nothing infectious, I hope? No germs floating about in the upstairs ether ...?'

'It's her nerves,' the man said. 'She's always been a nervy type.'

'I know she has, I don't need telling. Very highly strung, she is. Very what one might call *delicate*. So shall we pop upstairs and say hello? See your lady in her nightie?'

'Rather you didn't ...'

'She's had her wash, I take it? Because they get that smell when they stay in bed, that yeasty smell. All their hidden places start to pong a bit, which is fair enough, if you like that kind of thing. So I'm not complaining, though Billy might.'

'Maybe you should come back another time, then. Might be better.'

'It might be, Trevor, and it might not. You see, today is your day. I've set it aside specially, because I've been thinking of you, haven't I. Today, I told myself – while I shaved, before I showered, after I wanked – today belongs to Trevor.'

He undid the single button of his overcoat, letting it hang coyly open.

'So how's business, these days?'

'Not too good.'

The fatman shook his head, allowed himself a brief and rancid grin.

'Thought you'd say that. Can't imagine why.'

'It's true, Henry. No-one's buying.'

'So lower your prices. Cut the margin.'

'Couldn't pay the suppliers, I did that.'

'Fuck the suppliers, son. You've got to pay me.'

Henry sighed and glanced at his watch.

'I was meant to be somewhere else twenty minutes ago. You know that? I'm late for a previous engagement, because of you.'

Trevor blinked unhappily beneath the fluorescent light.

'My time's worth more than what you owe,' Henry said, 'but some things are more important than money. Principle is more important, and I'm a man of principle. I've got a tender heart, and I give a helping hand to people down on their luck. But I don't like being taken advantage of, do I. Never liked that, old son.'

He took out a packet of twenty.

'My fault, I suppose, cause I've always been good-natured.'

He tapped the base, and a couple of cigarettes poked up.

'Smoke?'

Trevor shook his head.

Henry lifted the pack to his mouth and slid a cigarette between his teeth.

'Don't be like that,' he said softly.

'Like what?'

'Unfriendly.'

The jeweller's skin turned unhealthily pale. He looked like a man who didn't eat his greens.

'I'm not really a smoker,' he explained quickly.

'That a fact.'

'My wife . . .' he said, 'she's always . . .'

'Shall I tell you something, Trevor?'

Henry struck a match.

'If I owed what you owe, and the man who lent it paid a visit,

I'd suck on a fag if he offered me one. I wouldn't purse my prissy lips and shake my head.'

He held the flame to the end of the weed.

'I mean I'd suck his fucking cock, if that would make him happy. That's what I'd do, Trevor. If you're interested.'

He blew a smooth plume of smoke into the air.

'It's called having social graces, old son.'

He took another drag, coughed it out, and glanced at the girl.

'How you doing, darling? Having fun?'

She gave a little nod, for she doesn't like to disappoint, she tries to be obliging. But having fun? Is she the type who goes through life aware of having *fun*? She's standing, quietly watching, conscious of the hum vibrating in the air, some discreetly watchful alarm system that has already sized her up, and marked her down, and found her rather wanting. For she gets these feelings, now and then. Feels dispossessed, like she's outside looking in, like a peasant at the gate.

'She's very quiet, isn't she, Trev? She ought to talk a bit more, or I'll start to wonder. Might start to think she's bored.'

He pushed his face right next to hers.

'You bored, then, are you? Cause if you are, my love, just let me know. Don't hesitate to mention it.'

And Donna, being prudent, says:

'Where's all the other customers, Henry?'

'There won't be any others, sweetheart, cause Trevor's locked the door. Better like that, get some privacy. Cause I like to do my shopping undisturbed, away from all the riff-raff. I keep my distance from the punters. Can't bear them, frankly. Smelly bastards. That right, Trevor? Am I right, Trev, eh?'

The jeweller nodded, even managed a smile. Henry clapped him on the shoulder. Not too hard, just nice and friendly.

'He's the boss round here, you know what I'm saying? He owns this place, he's not some flunky. Got a stake in this establishment. As has the bank, and diverse others. People who've lent him money, see. Soft-hearted types, like you-know-who. So he's not just nobody, is how I'd put it. He's not some piece of rubbish, is he?'

He let the statement hang in the air, and then he said:

'Forgive me, girls. I'm forgetting my manners. Allow me to do the introductions.'

He waved a hand.

'Sweetheart, this is Trevor. A business colleague, so to speak. Trevor, meet young precious. We've come to get her a bauble, Trev. Something bright and shiny. Nothing dull, OK? No antique silver for my girly. Something she can play with on a rainy afternoon.'

He glanced down into the nearest counter and pointed at a necklace made of thin silver chains.

'That'll do nicely, I'd have thought. Just right for little luscious.'

'My wife has one like that.'

'Does she really?'

'Silver's always been her weakness.'

'A very discerning lady.'

'Got quite a collection.'

'Nothing but the best, eh?'

'She knows how to keep herself,' the jeweller added.

'She does.' The fatman nodded gravely. 'She knows how to dress, your wife, I'll grant you that. Knows how to comb the hair and tie the scarf. A very elegant wife, she is. Very what I'd call *refined*. Hugely attractive and deeply seductive, the one you feed and bed, while she gives you head. Your charming lady wife, I know her rather well.'

He peered down at the necklace, eyes narrowing slightly.

'And I'm glad you're spending money on her. Shows you care, see? I like a bloke who spends on his wife. Even when he's in debt. Even when he can't pay what he owes, if he still keeps spending on his wife that makes me happy, Trevor. It makes my scrotum start to tingle, and I get a nice, warm feeling down below . . .'

The Henry smile.

'. . . which can't be bad.'

He pressed the tips of his fingers against cold plate glass.

'What's the damage then, Trev?'

'Well, normally . . .'

'To me, Trevor. What's the damage to me?'

'Three hundred.'

Henry emitted a low, mock-impressed whistle.

'And worth every penny, I shouldn't wonder. Only wish I could afford it. Would suit my little Donna, here.'

He gently stroked her cheek.

'Am I right, Trevor? You think she's worth three ton? Because I think she's worth it. I'd say three hundred quid to make her happy was what I'd call a bargain.'

He turned her round to face him, and let his eyes slide up and down. He gave the girl his full and frank attention.

'So speak up, sweetheart. Don't be shy. You want that thing, or not?'

She considered for a moment, cogitated carefully, and then she said:

'I think I'd rather not.'

'Too posh for you?'

'Too cheap.'

'Three ton, you tart.'

'It's not enough.'

'Joe couldn't buy it.'

'Not quite the point.'

He gazed at her for several moments.

'I prefer it when they're talkative.'

Smoothing his fingers along his lapel, playing with the end of his pointed lapel.

'Don't you love it, when they gab a bit? Can't beat it, can you, the lippiness of little girls. That's why we want them, eh, Trev? And when it gets too much we can shut the mouth, just stop it up, just shove the cork back in the bottle.'

And Donna, who has this streak in her, who lacks a sense of preservation, looks him in his fatman eye and says:

'I reckon you can't afford me.'

'I can afford anyone.'

'Almost anyone.'

'That's right, darling. Keep on gabbing.'

'Just a small-time crook.'

'Like kids, they are, when they get like this. Got to give them a smack when they get too cheeky.'

'Bit of thieving, bit of fencing, bit of lending on the side.'

'But they're delicate, see, so not too hard. Not in the face. I don't hit girlies in the face.'

'Bit of pimping, here and there.'

'Unless they really ask for it.' His tongue flicked out between his lips. 'Unless they really want it bad.'

'Toe-rag stuff, I would have thought.'

'You might be right,' he said, and slapped her twice with the back of his hand. Once on the cheek, once on the mouth, and each time the small and sated Henry grunt issued from his throat.

He examined her face, held it up to the light.

'Glad we've cleared the air,' he said. 'I'm feeling better, now.'

Her cheek had turned bright crimson, although he hadn't hit her hard, he thought. Not properly, just nice and gently. He watched the tears begin to flow, and knew what she was feeling: the shock, the pain, the lurching recognition that she's weightless in this world. He knew all that. He understood those things. He's an understanding man.

'You know something, Trevor? She's probably the type who doesn't like gifts. I mean some girls don't.'

He slipped a hand inside his coat and brought out an eight-inch hammer, being the sort who carries one around, as they often come in handy. He placed it gently on the counter.

'They'd rather their blokes were poor but honest, scratching a living in a Kilburn flat. Eating shit, and dressed in chainstore garbage. Always smiling, always ready to help the neighbours. Decent, wholesome blokes, God help us. They like them, Trevor, and it beats me why. Because a poor man's like a dead man, see? He's nothing, on this earth. So when a girly's being friendly to a corpse, it makes me wonder, sometimes. Makes me start to speculate. The ladies, son. I try and guess what makes them tick.'

He eased off his gloves and glanced at his watch.

'Running late now, Trev, so I think it's time I made my purchase.'

He took out his handkerchief and dabbed a tear from her swollen cheek. I'm kind, he thought. I'm a decent bloke.

'Turn off the bells,' he murmured. 'There's a good chap.'

The jeweller was staring at the hammer. It looked synthetic, somehow, lying on the counter, beside the fatman's hand. Unreal, beside the plump and hairless fingers.

'Pretty sharpish, if you wouldn't mind. Joey's on a double yellow, and you know the way he frets.'

'I'm sorry . . . ?'

'The alarm,' Henry clarified. 'Better switch it off, old mate. We don't want to wake up wifey.'

Trevor bent and reached under the counter. His skin was turning grey, he seemed almost to be shrivelling. It was as though the flesh were melting from his bones, as though he were retreating from this world. Tiny drops of moisture appeared, as if from nowhere, on his forehead. Maybe he was sweating. Maybe it was the light.

Henry picked up the hammer.

'Good lad,' he said.

She watched him move a few feet back. He raised his arm, seemed to half-run forward, and then, with a soft moan of pleasure, an exhalation of quiet contentment, he brought the hammer down, he swung it down, he slammed it very quickly down. Bright shards of glass arrowed into the air. The sound seemed to shatter inside her skull.

'I've always liked a noise,' he murmured. 'Bit of sound and fury.'

He reached inside, shoved away rings and bracelets, and plucked the silver necklace from the tray. He held it up and examined it carefully, turning it over to catch the light. The prize, he thought. The longed-for trophy. A modest gift for little girly.

'We'll take it as it is,' he said. 'You needn't wrap it.'

And he wished the jeweller all the best, took her firmly by the arm, and walked her through the door. By the time they reached the car, Joe had the engine running. Revs down low, just keeping it warm. Henry climbed in the back and pulled her down beside him, still gripping her tightly with his oldman's fingers.

'That's right, precious. Snuggle up close.'

The red mark on her face was already fading to a faint, becoming blush. It was almost gone, which he almost regretted.

Joe flicked off the radio and released the handbrake. He glanced in the mirror, waiting to be told.

'Back to me,' Henry ordered. 'She's coming to lunch.'

She took out her ciggies. (Camel Lights, her weed of choice.)

'I'm not hungry.'

He struck a match.

'You don't have to eat.'

She leaned towards the flame.

'I want to go to Kilburn.'

'What's wrong with Hampstead?'

She pressed a button. Her window slid down.

'Too green . . .'

She squinted up at the London sky.

'. . . too countrified.'

Joe held the clutch at biting point.

'Boss?'

The fatman sighed. She was a nylon type, not used to better things. Indulge her, for the moment.

'You saying you prefer his place to mine?'

'It's got more character.'

'Like damp and mould.'

'Yeah, stuff like that.'

Henry grunted. Made no difference, anyway. Take a bit longer, but same thing in the end.

'I like to please the ladies, Joe, can't bear it when they sulk. So just drop me off, OK? You take her back to you, and I'll come round later. Discuss some business, type of thing.'

He watched East Acton accelerate past the window.

'Might bring Mervyn,' he added, softly. 'Help pass the time.'

4

He cut open a tin of steak and kidney and emptied it into the saucepan. The girl was standing next to him, watching the mixture as it settled and spread.

'Nice necklace,' he commented.

'It's all right.' She passed him the plastic fork. 'Your boss gave it me.'

'That was generous.'

'He got it for nothing, anyway.'

Joe turned down the gas and began to stir.

'So did you.'

Early afternoon, and they're killing time till the fatman comes, waiting for Henry to pay them a visit. They'd both agreed she should stay a while, and she'd unpacked her things and stowed them away. The rain was sheeting down outside, thudding hard on the greasy pavement and bouncing off the basement steps. She switched off the gas.

'Shall I tell you something?'

'No, ta.'

'I don't know why you work for him.'

'It's a job,' he muttered.

'So's cleaning drains.'

He poured the brown stuff into a soup plate.

'You having some?'

She thought about it, for a nanosecond.

'You have it, Joe.'

'I don't mind sharing . . .'

She shook her head.

'You need your strength.'

She watched him pull out a chair and sit down at the table. He peeled some slices off the open loaf and started spooning up his lunch. He took his time, when he had his meals. Ate them slowly, with refinement. He might eat shit, she told herself, but he ate it like a prince. She idly wondered what Henry was having, what piece of prime-cut fillet was comfortably filling the Henry belly, what sated burp of satisfaction was softly parting his fatman lips.

'D'you also owe him?'

'Yeah.'

'Does everyone owe him?'

He tore a piece of bread in half and moved it slowly round the plate, soaking up gravy and bits of carrot.

'Yeah.'

He had peach slices for his afters, then went down the road to the mini-mart. Said he'd get some cake and things, some goodies for the fellers. He made her promise to fix the room, make it look its best, so she cleared the table and shifted some chairs. (Enough, she thought. Don't overdo it.) By the time her boy returned, the rain was easing off, the clouds were gradually parting. But even so, it was dark inside. No finger of light could poke inside a basement flat in Kilburn.

About ten past three the buzzer rang. Joe grinned his nervous, Joey grin. He smoothed down his hair and opened the door, and there they were, Merv and Henry, come to have their tea.

'Hello, son,' the fatman said, and stepped inside. He allowed his face to register the mildest distaste, the faintest suggestion that he might have seen better salons in his day.

'You've laid the table,' he noted. 'That's good,' he said. 'I like a man who uses doilies.'

His presence seemed to fill the room.

'Take a pew, Merv, that's the spirit. Make yourself at home, that's right. Joe won't mind, cause Joe's a pal.'

He spotted the girl. A flash of yellow smile.

'I grew up round here, can you believe it, eh? The fatman had a humble start. So I'm not a snob, in case you wondered. Might be a cunt, but I'm not a snob. That's why I like to come and visit. I just step inside the door and it all comes flooding back again: the filth of it, the shittiness. Makes me feel nostalgic, almost. I get this sort of tender wave inside my gut, and I think of my old man, poor bastard. My poor old dad, I think, the poor old fuck.'

He took off his coat, draped it over a chair.

'But nice little place you got here, Joe. Not too big, if you take my drift. What's known as *compact*, in the trade.'

He delicately sniffed the air.

'Got a pleasant whiff to it.'

A frown of concentration.

'I'd say you had braised beef and gravy for dinner. Some kind of stew, from some kind of can.'

He smacked his generous lips together, as if he wished

he'd been invited, as if it were his favourite meal.

'Am I right, Joe, eh? Tell me, Joey, am I right?'

He grinned at them. He was feeling good.

'Say something, why don't you.'

Joe patted the button-down sofa.

'Have a seat,' he suggested. 'Make yourself comfortable.'

'I will, son, don't you worry.'

He pulled out his handkerchief and whisked it neatly over the cushions. It was a habit of his, when making housecalls. In case of crumbs and things.

'Amazing what they can do with plastic, these days.'

He sat down carefully, squeezing his large buttocks onto the small seat.

'I mean it almost looks like leather, doesn't it? Not close up, of course, but when you're standing in the doorway, having a good look round. You're giving it the eyeball, and you see this big thing shining in the light, and fuck me, you think, Joey's got a leather sofa. The toe-rag's living well, you think.'

He pulled one of the cups towards him and filled it with dark brown liquid.

'And then you step inside, and you come up close, and you relax a bit, you unwind a bit, you calm down a bit, because it's only plastic, isn't it? Cause Joe can't pay his rent, and when you live on tick you shouldn't sit on leather. Shouldn't park your arse on hand-stitched hide when you've still got bills to pay.'

A dash of milk, two lumps of sugar.

'You ought to squat on the ground, if I'm being honest. Ought to sit on the pavement, just sit in a puddle on the fucking pavement. That's what you ought to do, Joe. That's my honest opinion, for what it's worth, which isn't much.'

He took a cautious sip and nodded to the girl.

'Nice spot of tea, this, sweetheart. Is it Darjeeling?'

With which remark he paused and drained his cup. No

sound, save that of liquid going down the gullet. So not quite silence, but very nearly. He was feeling mellow, quite at ease, the tannin warmth cascading through his belly. He leaned back in the sofa and flicked his gaze around the room.

'If I had to find a term for it, I'd call this flat *appropriate*. You've found your niche, my boy. You've found your place in life.'

He picked up a chocolate digestive.

'Just open the window, now and then.'

Allowed himself a generous bite.

'Lift the sash and let some air in. Make a pleasant change.'

Washed it down with a glass of squash.

'You're getting like my clients, Joe. I mean I go and see them, and their rooms smell bad. They haven't heard about open windows, they don't believe in London breezes. What might be termed as common types, just rubbish, really, just hoi polloi. They sit inside all day and breathe stale air. They rub and sweat and touch themselves, and forget about their creditors. You should leave it open, I tell them. An hour or so a day, and you get your circulation. Fresh air won't hurt you, I tell them. Billy might, but fresh air won't.'

And then he laughed, to let them know he was only joking, and cut himself a generous slice of lemon sponge.

'Give me a break,' Joe said. 'Be reasonable.'

'People are always saying that, son. What they usually mean is they can't make the payments. They don't say it right out like that. They never say it straight out. They circle round it, like it could burn them. Be reasonable, they say. Like I'm a mug.' He peered at Joe. 'You think I'm a mug?'

Joe shook his head.

'Didn't quite catch that.'

'No, boss.'

'No boss. I'm not a mug. I'm not soft, see, nor am I stupid.

I'm the man who lent you money. I'm the man, the reasonable man, you came to when you had a problem. I need a grand, boss. Lend me a grand, boss. And did I keep you waiting? Did I say, Not now, come back next month? Did I try and tell you times were hard? Did I?'

'No, boss.'

'I handed it over. Just like that. Without arguing. Without quibbling. Without asking for collateral. And you know why I don't ask for collateral?'

'No, boss.'

'Because you *are* the collateral. And your mum. And the little bit of lusciousness who's sitting by your side.'

'Give me another week, that's all.'

'I've always been soft like that. They come to me, these people, these types who can't get credit when everyone can get credit, when children can get credit, they come to me and they say, Help me, Henry. Tide me over. And out of my good nature, my limitless compassion, I say, What do you want, pal? You name it, I say, and you've got it. You want a grand? You've got a grand. And I never say when I want it back. I never tell them I need it back by a certain date. I don't even *give* them a fucking date. So they never have to pay it back, unless they really want to. All they have to pay is the five per cent. Five per cent, per week, every week, is all they have to pay. And I explain this to them. I sit them down and explain it to them, and I let them decide if they want my dough. And if they do, if they go away and think about it and come back and say, Henry, you're the lender for me, all I get is a verbal agreement. There's nothing to sign, see. I don't take their pension books, their child allowance books, nothing like that. Because I'm a man of principle. I just hand over the money and we shake on it and they give me their word they'll come through each week. Their word is their bond, I tell myself. Sound people, I tell myself. A promise made is a promise kept, I tell myself. Am I right?'

'Yeah, but . . .'

'So if someone takes my money, freely takes my money, and all I want is the interest, the percentage interest he agreed to pay, the five per cent he gave his word he'd pay, is that unreasonable? Is it? I'm asking.'

'It's not.'

'Too right, it's not. What's unreasonable is some people, people who don't open their windows, people who live in smelly flats, thinking they don't have to pay what they ought to pay. People who think they're Brazil. That's what I call unreasonable.'

Joe shifted in his chair.

'You know you'll get it,' he muttered.

'I know that, son. I just don't know when. And it's the when that counts, see. It's the when that matters.'

Henry wiped his fingers on a paper napkin.

'Don't tell me you can't manage, that's all. Just go for a walk one night, stick your fist through a car window and take the stereo. Then sell it down the pub. Then do the same the next night, and the night after that, until you've got enough to pay what you owe. Then whatever you make will be profit. Whatever you make, you'll be getting ahead. You've got a duty to your lady, Joe, and you're falling down on your duty. You've got to feed her, clothe her, get a decent car, live in a better neighbourhood, mix with smarter people. You've got to start acting like you're someone, Joe. Start taking what you need, and then you'll get respect.'

Henry paused for breath. Good speech that, he told himself. Deserves appreciation. He glanced at Mervyn, but Mervyn wasn't listening. Mervyn was eating custard creams, to which he seemed quite partial. Joe was staring at the carpet, saying nothing, there being nothing much to say. Donna was bending over the table, stacking dishes, nice and docile.

The fatman picked up his empty plate.

'Want some help, there, darling?'

Moving swiftly across the carpet. Very light on his feet, for such a heavy man. Very quick off the mark, for such a bulky chap. She brushed past him.

'No.'

He followed her into the kitchen.

'It's no bother,' he said. 'I like mucking in.'

He watched her hold each dish under the cold tap for a few seconds.

'That how you wash up?'

She shook water off her hands.

'Domesticated, aren't you?' he observed. He passed her the dishcloth. 'Make someone a nice little housekeeper.'

He bent towards her.

'You ever need a job,' he said, 'you know where to come.'

The milky breath in her face.

'Excuse me,' she said.

She stepped past him and began stacking crockery in a plastic rack.

He took her by the waist and turned her round to face him.

'Just for once,' he said, 'just for today,' he said, 'I want you to pretend you like me.'

She gazed at him for several seconds.

'But I don't like you, Henry.'

And something flickered in his eyes, but he kept on smiling. He lifted her chin and kissed her wetly on the mouth, and she felt the warm sweat on his face and the hard bulge between his legs.

'That's my girl,' he smiled. 'My Donna-girl.'

Pressing up so tight she had to brace herself against the wall to shove him off. She wiped her mouth with the back of her hand.

'Don't be like that,' he said quietly. 'Be nice, you bitch.'

He wrapped his fingers round her wrist.

'So fucking snotty, aren't you?'

He twisted her arm. Not too hard, not enough to break it, just enough to hurt her. Just enough to give the bitch some pain.

'I mean, a shitty bedsit off Kilburn Lane, and she thinks she's found a future.'

He felt her try to wriggle free. No strength, he thought. Like holding a bird.

'He's a driver, darling, so he's rubbish, see? Can't even keep you in tampons, can he? Just a sad little bastard who'll buy you fuck all.'

It gave him pleasure, to feel her struggle. So slim, she was. Such a bit of nothing. It pleasured him, enormously. The bitch, he thought. The luscious bitch.

'D'you like poor blokes, then? Cause there's a lot of them around, sugar. Blokes like him, see. Blokes who want to stick it in for nothing. All cock and no cash, darling, that what you like?'

'You can't imagine what I like.'

'Try me.'

'You think money's everything.'

'I know it, sweetheart. I know it absolutely. It's the iron law of life: if you don't have it, you get shafted.'

And he let her go, watched her rub her dainty skin. Not his fault, he told himself. She made him, frankly. She wound him up. He brushed his sleeve and flicked a speck of vagrant sponge to the floor.

'I just don't think you need a dosser, that's all.'

'He's one of your boys, Henry.' She wiped a teaspoon on

the cloth. 'I thought you looked after your boys.'

'I do, my love. Long as they're loyal.'

She chucked the cloth on to the draining board.

'Only dogs are loyal.'

The fatman smiled.

'My boys are dogs.'

He leaned forward and turned off the tap, for he liked to make a contribution, he liked to do his bit.

'Look,' he said, 'let's be friends, all right? Joe's basically a mate, so you be nice to me, and I'll be nice to him.'

'How nice?'

'He owes twelve-fifty.'

'Much as that?'

'I'll wipe it.'

'Because he's a mate . . .'

'Because you'll be nice.'

He watched her think it over, could see the Donna cogs revolving in her brain.

'He's a soft lad, see. Needs cherishing.'

He opened one of the cupboards and began to root inside.

'Been bullied a bit,' he murmured. 'Schoolboy stuff, but pretty nasty.'

A small exclamation of pleasure as he found a pack of assorted wafers.

'You want to know what they did?'

'Not really.'

'Because I'll tell you if you want.'

'Rather you didn't.'

'Well as you're asking, as you're begging: they tied a ribbon round his thing and pulled him round the playground. In front of everyone, can you believe that, eh? I mean *kids*, I ask you.'

He leaned towards her and lowered his voice.

'Between ourselves, of course. I mean he told me that in confidence.'

And he tapped the side of his nose and chewed on a caramel wafer. The girl began edging past.

'Going back in, are we? Allow me, darling.'

He held the door open and went in after her.

'Been having a chin-wag,' he announced. 'Bit of a chat with little luscious.'

'We off soon?'

'You bored, then, Merv?'

'I've got this date, see.'

A spasm wrenched the fatman's gut, for it always disturbed him, when the boys did that, when they showed their true, unfettered natures, revealed their damp and clammy urges. It pained him in his lower belly, made his insides throb and burn, and he'd have to take some milk to cool them down.

'Delighted for you. A girly, is it?'

'In her thirties.'

'Not like you, son, to be so generous.'

'Make better fucks, boss. More grateful, aren't they?'

'Well spotted, Merv, and this is tremendous news. Am I right, Joe, eh? You happy for him? Cause I am, see. I'm a happy man.'

The ache inside his fatman gut, and Henry had this sudden longing to be physical, to unburden all his Henry stress, relieve himself by doing something dirty. A need he had. He couldn't help it. To feed the need was all he wanted.

He beckoned them over, the three of them. Merv and Joe and Donna, him and him and her.

'I want to tell you people something.'

He took out a box of slim panatellas.

'So gather round, cause it's interesting.'

He permitted Merv to light one for him, for rank must have its privilege.

'You see,' he explained, 'there are two types of man on this brutal earth: the ones who are bent and shafted, and the ones who do the shafting. So when you're me – what's known in the trade as the Henry type – you can basically do what you want in life. You can please yourself, more or less. You can treat your friends like the filth they are, and they'll thank you for it. They'll bow the knee, and bend the head, and press their eager faces to your groin.'

He spat out a fragment of green-brown leaf.

'Or that's what I've always found,' he murmured. 'Though I might be wrong.'

He gazed at the girl.

'I'm going to prove something to you, sugar, so bear with me, OK? But before I start, you've got to understand my basic premise: these lads you like – it's all show, see? Big, strong lads, and they're girlies inside. Just acting, aren't they. Just having you on. So every time you see them strut, every time they look you in the eye, let you think they'll do the business, just bear in mind they're just pretending. Cause deep down, sweetheart, buried within their wild-boy hearts, all they want is peace and quiet . . .'

He dragged the smoke inside his lungs.

'. . . and somewhere warm so they can menstruate.'

He flicked some ash to the floor, and then he said:

'A moment, Joe, if you wouldn't mind.'

He waved him over, had him come and stand beside him. Then he nodded, almost imperceptibly, and Mervyn, who was used to this, who'd done it once or twice before, grabbed Joe from behind, so that Henry, with his longing to be physical, to unburden all his Henry stress, could relieve himself by doing something dirty. A need he had. He couldn't help it. To feed the need was all he wanted.

'The joys of being me,' he said, 'the sweet and wholesome pleasures.'

And he slowly slid his hand across Joe's thigh, until it came to rest right on his crotch, his private parts, his pure and perfect genitals.

'For when you're me,' he said, 'when you've got the great good fortune to be me,' he said, 'you can do this sort of thing.'

'I think he's partial,' Mervyn breathed.

'You reckon?'

'Yeah.'

The fatman thought it over.

'It's important, Merv. It makes a difference. I mean the question is,' he said, 'the question surely is,' he said, 'does he like it? Cause if he does, he's laughing. If he does, we're doing him a favour, we're giving him some pleasure, we're merely being friendly.'

He closed his fingers round the lump. Not too hard, just nice and gently. And Joey standing there, his arms pinned back behind him, with that Joey grin spread on his face, mutely watching while Henry fondled, quietly waiting while he had a fumble. Just standing, big and stupid, while Henry did his Henry stuff.

'I can do what I like,' the fatman said. He gave another squeeze. 'That's my basic trouble.'

Mervyn looked at the girl and a thought occurred.

'D'you think she'd like some too?'

His thin, wet tongue.

'Cause I think she might. I mean she looks so full of herself.'

'She does.'

'And she could be full of me.'

'She could.'

'So shall I, then?'

'Better not,' the fatman said. 'He might not like it.'

'Fair point.'

'And we better not wind up Joey-boy.'

'Be hell to pay.'

'Have to go into hiding.'

'The fear,' Merv said, 'I'd be sick with it . . .'

'Just vomit it up.'

'Joe on the rampage.'

'With his slow grin, and his soft cock . . .'

'That's the feller.'

'Thought it might be,' Henry murmured. 'Some girls, though, they prefer them like that.'

'Like what?'

'Like that. Sweet-natured boys with gentle lips. Tender lads who can't protect them. As if there's nothing bad, out there. As if you can walk down the road with a gutless man, and God will protect you.'

'As if . . .'

'Because they don't like men with balls, any more. Not big, round balls they can kiss every night. Not ballsy men. Not men like me.'

Because that's what Henry doesn't get, he can't understand their reasoning. Incomprehension, to be frank. Something there's eluding him.

'Because me,' he said, 'a man like me, a large and vicious man like me, I mean me,' he said, 'that's only fair. Because I fuck them till they fall asleep, sweet and hard and in the hole. I stuff them till they've had enough, just shove it in and move it round, just do it till I've shut them up. So me,' he said, 'if they fell for me . . .'

'Make a lot of sense.'

'Be logical.'

Joe and Donna. Weightless, in this world.

'You know something, Merv? Some bird once said to me, some tart with a heart, some cunt from social services, she said, Why do you do these things, Henry? What things? I said. The things you do, she said. Because I can, I said. Oh, she said.'

Mervyn shook his head.

'They don't understand, do they?'

Henry nodded.

'Very slow on the uptake.' He removed his hand from Joey's bulge. 'We're going now, Merv.'

'Now, you mean?'

'You got a date, son.'

Mervyn grinned.

'Oh yeah, I forgot.'

'Must have been all the excitement.'

'Must have.'

'So like I said . . .' Henry smiled at her. The fatman charm. 'Come round tomorrow, about four o'clock. We'll start again. Be friends, OK?'

He picked up his coat.

'We'll have some tea and take it slowly. No hassle, right? You be nice to me, and I'll be nice to him, OK? All for one, and one for all.'

'I saw that film.'

'It was good, eh, Merv?'

'It was brilliant, boss.'

5

She pulled on her gloves.

'It suits you, this car.'

He changed down to second, surged past a lorry.

'I know.'

Rain spattered onto the windscreen.

'Suits you more than it suits him.'

He flicked on the intermittent wipe.

'I know.'

She stared out of the window.

'You ever wonder, Joey, what it's like, to be like that?'

'Like what?'

'Like him, Joe. What it's like to be like him.'

They were passing through the back end of Kensal Rise.
She'd been to a party round there once, a packed and raucous

party, given by a guy called Tom. A sudden, fleeting memory of calvados and endless food.

'I mean he ponces round,' she said, 'all fat, all rich . . .'

'Can't help his size.'

'. . . always bragging . . .'

'He likes to talk.'

'. . . always sneering . . .'

'A very wordy man.'

'. . . all mouth,' she said, 'all fucking mouth.'

'He reads a lot.' Joe shrugged. 'They get like that.'

He hung a right into Chevening Road. They were digging it up down the left-hand side, and the cars were stacked up thirty yards back. There was a lot of noise, for such a little street. A lot of sound, if you were listening.

He stuck two ciggies in his mouth.

'You going to let him . . . ?'

'Let him what?'

'Let him you know.'

She turned in the seat so she could see his face.

'You think I'd do that, to wipe your debt?'

'Be a thoughtful gesture.'

'You're not funny, Joe.'

He got out his lighter.

'But I look good, don't I.'

He lit the ciggies and passed one over.

'So what'll you do, then, when he tries?'

She switched on the heater and turned it to max.

'I'll improvise.'

They ploughed on up through Brondesbury, and the houses got bigger, the hedges higher. Different route, same destination. Twelve more minutes, and they're pulling up in Henry's drive, getting his gravel stuck in the tyres. He swung the car round so it was facing the road. She watched him cut the motor, listened to the engine ticking.

'You'll be out here, right?'

He nodded.

'Right.'

'Cause I'm doing it for you, Joe, aren't I.'

He stared at the bonnet.

'Doing what, exactly?'

'Sorting things out.'

'So you're going to let him.'

'I'm going to sort things out.'

She unclipped the belt.

'If you hear any screams . . .'

He shoved open his door.

'I'll run for help.'

He heaved himself out and came round the other side, shielding his hair from gusting rain. He was polite like that, being well brought up. He'd always make sure that he helped the lady. He turned up her collar and touched her cheek.

'I'll be waiting, OK?'

'Keep it warm for me, Joe.'

'I'll do that,' he promised. 'The engine too.'

She began walking up the drive towards the redbrick house, the solid, bourgeois, bay-fronted villa, that Henry had made his home. She placed her finger on the button and heard a bell inside. There wasn't a nameplate to guide the perplexed, no printed sign that the fatman lived there. There should have been, she thought. There ought to be some indication, perhaps a piece of paper stuck beside the letterbox on which was written: *Here Lives A Cunt*. Might have helped, she reasoned. Might have been of interest to the casual passer-by.

She rang again. The intercom crackled on.

'Yes?'

Billy's voice, lisping down the wire.

'It's me,' she said.

The Donna Bitch, she could have added. The sacrificial lamb, the mutely uncomplaining morsel, the piece of sweetly perfumed flesh for Henry's delectation.

There was an electronic whirr and the steel-backed door swung open. Joe had told her about that door. It was a special, Henry kind of door. You put your key in the middle, and you turned it twice, and four steel bolts shot neatly out, locking into the corners of the frame. So you couldn't get in uninvited, couldn't smash the locks and kick it down, go barging your way inside. You'd have to burn an oxy-hole, have to bring the gear and concentrate, and it makes a row and it takes for ever. But that's bosses for you, Joe concluded. That's how they live, see. Tucked away and out of reach.

Billy appeared in the porch, blocking the way, his pitted face consumed with doubt.

'Expecting you, is he?'

He was picking at his rash. Not scratching it, exactly, just playing with his favourite spots.

'I think he is, Billy,' she said. 'I'd have thought he's in a state of fairly high expectation, if you really want to know.'

She watched him scrape a fingernail across his cheek, sending flakes of dead skin floating down onto the tiles.

'So better let me in, my love. Don't keep the big man waiting.'

He watched her silently for several seconds, observed her closely with his bleached-out eyes. The rain began slapping on the gravel. She could smell the wetness in the air.

'Bit nippy out here.' She hunched into her coat. 'Be a gent, why don't you.'

Some sound came from the back of his throat, some phlegm-embellished statement of his feelings, and he moved reluctantly aside. She stepped past him into the lobby. Mervyn was lounging against a hall table, legs crossed at the ankles, hands plunged deep in trouser pockets.

'Hello, darling. Come for a job?'

'Something like that.'

'Because we've got a cleaner already,' he said. 'We've got a woman who does.'

'Does what?'

'She does everything.'

'That's nice.'

'Certainly is.'

Billy pushed the door shut and came over. Eyeing her warily, like she was some disease.

'We taking her up, then?'

'Not yet,' Mervyn said. 'Make her wait a bit.'

'What for?'

'Good for her character.'

He waved a hand towards a Dralon chair in the corner.

'Have a seat, sugar. Give your feet a rest.'

'I think we should take her up,' Billy urged.

Mervyn shook his head.

'She's too early, Billy.'

The skinhead frowned.

'Why's she early, Merv?'

'Because she's eager, son.'

Billy gazed at her.

'We don't like it when they're eager, do we.'

'Bit off-putting,' Merv agreed.

'Bit slaggy, frankly, and we don't like slags.'

Mervyn tilted his head, in the mood for reminiscence.

'I had my first one down in Cornwall.'

'That was very rural of you.'

'She was so relaxed, down there.'

'In Cornwall, you mean?'

'In her lower parts.'

'Her nether regions . . .'

'They're the ones. I didn't realize at the time, of course. But then I wouldn't, would I? Being young, and being as it was my first. Only realized later, once I'd been in other ones, and it occurred to me she might have been unusual. So loose, she was, so overstretched, I hardly felt a thing.'

'I think I might have met her sister . . .'

Billy squinted at the ceiling. He screwed his eyes against the light, and tried to recollect.

'. . . a pleasant girl, but cavernous.'

'She made me kiss her down below.'

'On her thing?'

'Had no choice. She spread her legs and shoved my face right in, the dirty cow.'

'The filthy sow.'

Mervyn sighed.

'I was only fourteen.'

'Poor sod.'

'Precisely.'

The rain was sheeting down outside. It was bouncing off the porch and hissing on the gravel.

'I gave her something, after.'

'A dose, I hope.'

'My dad said always show you're grateful.'

'Your *dad* said that?'

'So I gave her a fiver . . .'

'To please your dad.'

'. . . and then she hit me.'

'Should have made it ten.'

'You reckon?'

'Yeah.'

Mervyn brooded on his misspent youth.

'But she wasn't worth ten,' he pointed out. 'And if they're not worth ten, you shouldn't give them ten.'

'You should give them seven-fifty.'

'You should give them fuck all.'

They stood there, for a moment, in mute and pained agreement. Slowly Merv uncrossed his legs. His joints felt stiff. The damp, he thought. This filthy weather. He glanced at the girl.

'Don't mind us,' he said. 'Just having a chat, see. Bit of lad-talk, sort of thing.'

He shifted his weight, got off the table.

'And might I add how ravishing you're looking? That right, Billy? Wouldn't you say that girly's looking scrumptious?'

They came and stood in front of her, gazing down.

'Nice lipstick,' Mervyn said.

'It's very red,' the skinhead added.

'More like pink.'

'It's very pink.'

'And it's very nice.'

Billy frowned.

'She's looking kind of . . .'

Mervyn nodded.

'Isn't she.'

He peered a little closer.

'Do you think she's had her shower?'

'Today, you mean?'

'Because he doesn't like them *over*-clean. He's not obsessive, as he puts it. Prefers them in their natural state. Likes it when they've got that *whiff*.'

'Not smelly . . . ?'

'No. Just earthier.'

He cleared his throat and sniffed the air around her head.

'So he won't be pleased, then.'

'We should have told her.'

'Might have helped.'

Merv bent and stared, came right up close, could have pressed his putrid flesh against her cheek.

'She's all right, isn't she.'

'Very tasty.'

'Reckon there's enough, though?'

'Enough of what?'

'To go round, I mean.'

'Bit coarse, there, Merv, but I take your point.'

'I thought you might. Cause first there was Joe, and now there's Henry, and what I'd like to know, the thing I'd really like to know, is—'

'What about us?'

'Exactly.'

'Cause we've got feelings too.'

'We have.'

Their scrubbed and shining faces hovered above her head. Merv and Billy being friendly, exuding laddish bonhomie.

A hand reached forward, plump and hairless. They hadn't heard him coming down. Fleshy men are like that, sometimes. They can creep along, they can shift their weight without a sound, so that one minute they're upstairs, awaiting little luscious, and the next they're down here in the hallway, bending Billy's ear.

'My lady and I,' he was speaking slowly, 'don't wish to be disturbed.'

He clamped his fingers on the skinhead lobe and began to twist it round.

'That clear, son, is it? Cause if it's not, please let me know. If I'm not completely bell-like in my clarity, just give a nod, just pass the word, and I'll try to make amends.'

Billy's pinkly insubstantial face had pulled into a grin of pain.

His mouth hung loosely open, the tongue flopped out, saliva bubbles formed and burst.

He's right, she thought. His boys are dogs.

The fatman took her by the hand.

'Glad you came,' he murmured.

He began to lead his guest upstairs.

'And I trust you're going to enjoy your visit, because if you don't enjoy it, I won't enjoy it.'

His face was glistening in the light. You could have sucked his cheek, were you so inclined. Could have licked the sweat with your Donna tongue.

'Or more precisely,' he explained, 'I won't enjoy it *quite* as much, for buried somewhere in my brain I'll know my chosen lady of the day, the current queen of my desire . . .'

He paused for breath.

'. . . is lying, sulking, underneath.'

They climbed two flights and stopped in front of a panelled door. He stood beside her, soft and panting.

'So make an effort, is what I'm saying.'

A gracious Henry smile.

'It's only manners, after all.'

6

She'd never entered an old man's bedroom before, and a frisson of non-excitement, a gentle wave of premature ennui, engulfed her. This was where he lived and had his being, where he took himself in hand and stroked himself to sleep.

'Have a seat, why don't you.'

He nodded towards the mammoth bed, with its freshly laundered linen. So nothing too offensive there, nothing stale about the sheets. She keeps an eye on things like that, for she won't be soiled by Henry's sheets. By Henry, maybe, but not his sheets.

'Stretch out on the bed, why don't you. Relax a bit, see if the mattress suits.'

'Looks fine to me.'

'Test it, just in case.'

'In case of what?'

'In case you'd prefer the floor.' He opened a walnut cabinet. 'Like a drink, then, sweetheart?'

He peered inside.

'We got whisky, brandy, bit of lemon vodka. Some Babycham for the ladies, Bacardi and coke for the slags.'

He opened a bottle of single malt.

'Good stuff, this.' He took a long sniff. 'Helps the juices flow.'

He poured out amber liquid and held up the glass. She shook her head.

'Bit early, thanks. But you go ahead.'

He took a slug, and she glanced around. It seemed a very Henry kind of room, thick with wood and dank with age. A packed and gloomy oldman room, and she loathed it, absolutely. She would have trashed the place, if she'd had the chance, just burnt it down and walked away. Just wrecked it, if she could, for that's the kind of girl she is.

'Nice,' she murmured.

A blush of satisfaction spread across his neck.

'You like it . . . ?'

'Mmmmm. It's very *you*.'

Looking pleased with this, looking gratified, he beckoned her over to the coffee table. It was laid for two, with bread and honey and a jug of hot milk. He poured out a steaming cupful, a look of quiet contentment on his face.

'Want some, do you?'

The skin, she thought. He drinks the *skin*.

'I'd rather not.'

'It settles the stomach.'

'I think I'll pass.'

He tore off a piece from a long baguette.

'You're like my boys,' he muttered. 'Don't know what you're missing.'

66

He compressed the bread between his fingers, and dipped it into the liquid.

'You want to try it, sometime. Might calm you down.'

He placed the sodden morsel on his tongue. For several seconds, no sound but that of mastication, of Henry getting pleasure. Then he drained the cup and licked his lips, and a small, white blob of milky bread rolled down his chin.

'Can I ask you something?'

She nodded.

'Course.'

'You're fond of Joe, right?'

'We have our moments.'

''Cause it's beyond me, see, how blokes like him contrive to get their women.'

'He's a looker, Henry.'

'But he's poor, my love, and like I always say, a poor man's like a dead man. He's insubstantial, isn't he? Not a lot of *presence*, really. So a girl who goes with a bloke like that, she's letting a kind of corpse inside, she's communing with the dear departed. And that's not nice, in my opinion. That's not what I'd call wholesome, frankly.'

'He's got his good points.'

'Yeah? Like what?'

'He's kind and gentle.'

Henry snorted.

'So's Larry Lamb. So's Andy fucking Pandy.'

'No need to shout.'

'Can't help it, darling. I've got this cock, see, and we're like that, sometimes. Blokes, I mean. The three-legs of this world. We get aggressive, from time to time, and if your Joey doesn't, he's not what I'd call blokey, sweetheart. Not quite a lad.'

He wiped his mouth.

'Bit wimpy, really.'

With which acute remark, he got to his feet and unzipped his flies. A shade optimistic, possibly, but she felt it prudent not to say. He pulled down his trousers, peeled off his shirt and stood there, waiting, by the bed. It was an opportune moment to have a good look. The boss of bosses had off-white panties, pouting nipples, and a look of expectation on his face. There was a modest amount of body hair. Just enough for decency, not quite enough for potency. But he passed the Donna test, for she's never liked them smooth. If you like them smooth, she's always thought, you really want a girly.

He slipped a hand inside his pants and moved it gently round. 'It's OK, precious. Only checking.'

She had a sudden, urgent need to avert her eyes, and her gaze alighted on the bedside table. She looked again, just to be sure, and there it was: pure loveliness, sheer poetry. For the first time since she'd stepped inside, she was seeing what truly excited her, and her dormant passion began to stir.

'What's that money, Henry?'

'What money, sugar?'

'By the bed, Henry.'

'That's yours, my love.' He moved a little nearer. 'A wodge of notes in your sticky hand, for services as yet unrendered.'

'So apart from wiping Joey's debt . . .'

'You get a bonus.'

'Oh.'

She gazed with fondness at the waiting pile. Small, brown tenners, and large, blue twenties, and a few sweet fivers, just for luck. A thick, little heap of unused notes. All mine, she thought, with a sudden rush of self-esteem. For me, she thought. Because I'm nice.

He pulled her close, pressed his mouth against her neck, then reached behind and cupped the tender Donna rump inside the velvet jeans.

'Be good,' he said, 'you just be nice, and the fatman will take care of you. Because I've always been quite kind like that, been generous to my ladies.'

He eased his groin against her crotch.

'I like to keep them happy.'

'How happy, Henry?'

She reached towards the beckoning notes.

His full lips parted. The Henry smile.

'Not quite yet,' he said, and clamped his sweaty fingers round her wrist.

'I think we're being somewhat previous. Somewhat premature, in fact.'

He pulled her arm away.

'First we get friendly, and then we get paid.'

His face was filmed with perspiration, the eyes a pale and washed-out grey, like an English sky in winter.

'So if you'd care to get undressed, I'd be obliged.'

So close he was, all milkiness and drooping age.

'Rather not,' she said, 'for the moment.'

She took a step back. An apologetic smile.

'Bit prim, you see. Bit ill at ease.'

'Won't take long,' he promised. 'Be over in a jiffy.'

'Another time, perhaps.'

'Don't like it when you're difficult.'

'Doctor's orders, I'm afraid.'

'Cause if you're going to be difficult, I'll have to be firm.'

'I'm allergic, see . . .'

Her brain moved fast.

'. . . to sperm.'

He paused.

'You mean the creamy stuff . . . ?'

'The very same.'

Which shut him up for a good few seconds. He sucked his

teeth and gazed at her. He fixed her with his piggy eye.

'You're serious, right? Not having me on? Cause I'm quite devoid of humour, where my privates are concerned.'

'I'm sure you are, and I wouldn't dare.'

He was looking doubtful.

'Why'd you come here, then?'

'Because you asked me, Henry. For tea,' she added. 'Scones and things. Toast and honey and Radio Four.'

'Honey?'

'Yeah.'

'In luck, then, aren't you.'

He picked up the jar and examined the label.

'Marks & Sparks. That good enough?'

'It's *lovely*,' she breathed. 'You're a *very* sweet man.'

'I know I am.' He peeled off his pants. 'Can't help it, really.'

And he stood before her, completely naked, pink and gleaming in the light. Oh shit, she thought. Oh buggeration. He passed her the jar and a silver teaspoon.

'You smearing, then?'

'*You* smear, Henry. I'm too excited.'

He led her into the bathroom, an endless expanse of chrome and tile, and perched his frame on a wooden stool. Unscrewing the lid, for she likes to be helpful, she placed the jar on the laundry box.

'I'm glad we've got that sorted,' he muttered, 'because I made it all nice, even changed the sheets.'

Grunting slightly as he leaned his weight forward, he dipped his hand in the open jar and scooped out a generous glob. Then he parted his legs and anointed himself, spreading it over the purple sack, the veined and baggy Henry pouch, which contained his modest orbs. The slap of skin on tender skin. The pleasures of the flesh.

'For you, this is,' he reminded her. 'So come on, darling . . .'

He sucked his fingers, one by one.

'. . . make an old man happy.'

She gazed, entranced, at the glistening mess. The words 'horrified fascination' slipped, unbidden, into her brain. Henry was dripping on the floor. His belly hung discreetly down, not quite obscuring the bits and bobs, the moist and waiting succulence, that nestled coyly between his thighs. The air, she realized, smelled of milk and honey. She had reached her promised land.

'You're looking good,' she commented. 'Looking really yummy, Henry.'

She stared at him, and knew she couldn't do it. Not for Joe. Not even for money, and she'd always been quite keen on money.

'Suppose I'd better get undressed, then, hadn't I.'

She edged towards the doorway.

'Pin my hair up, type of thing.'

He scratched his armpit.

'I'll be waiting, sugar.'

She blew him a kiss.

'Don't start without me.'

She stepped into the bedroom and closed the door, her Donna heart pulsating in her chest. Had she been the type who sweats, one might have noticed perspiration. The cash still waited on the bedside table. It was hers, she reasoned. She'd done her bit, she'd earned it, fair and square. She'd watched him spreading honey on his thingy, so the dosh belonged to her.

She smoothly palmed the notes and stuffed them in her bag. A couple of minutes was what she reckoned. Two clear minutes before a sudden roar of comprehension, a bellow of slick and dripping rage, would bring the minions running.

She left the bedroom and padded along the corridor. She

hoped there wouldn't be a scene, no confrontation, or other aggravation. She began to make her way downstairs. Don't run, she thought, for ladies never run. Girlies might, but ladies don't. Down the first flight, along the landing, down the second, and she's nearly there. Joey outside, and she's nearly there. She rounded the bend, and:

'My, my, my . . .'

Merv was standing in the hall, leaning against the steel-backed door. Gloomy down there, just a single bulb. The fatman saving pennies. He watched her coming down the stairs.

'She does look well.'

Hands sunk deep in trouser pockets, and that look on his face, that Mervyn smirk.

'Bit flushed, perhaps.' He narrowed his eyes. 'Bit pink of cheek.'

She reached the bottom and he moved towards her.

'But it suits you, sweetheart, so don't be shy.'

The rosebud mouth approached her ear.

'Had our tea, then, have we?'

He grabbed the flesh of her upper arm. Enough to hurt, though not to bruise.

'Had our bite of sticky bun?'

His face pushed up so close, she could see the blackheads round his nose, the fresh, new cold sore on his upper lip.

'Got a problem, Merv?'

'No problem, sugar.'

His eyes slid slowly up and down, took in the tight, black jeans, the three-inch heels, the low-cut top. Looking good, the boy was thinking. The Donna bitch was looking good.

Muffled banging from upstairs, the sound of wardrobes being searched and trashed. She gently pulled away.

'Better dash, sweetie. Boss might want you.'

He drew back the bolts and opened the door, and she went before him, out of the darkness and into the light.

'Next time you come to visit,' he said, 'try and save some for the boys.'

The fleeting Donna smile.

'I'll do that, Merv. Believe me.'

7

She didn't like to move too much, if she could possibly avoid it, but when she left that house, she came out running.

It was late on a frozen afternoon, and the cold so bitter that had she been the weepy type she would have wept. The wind came slicing down the road and cut into her face. It made her skull begin to hurt, and her teeth begin to ache, and forced her lips so far apart you might have looked at her and thought that she was grinning, you might have thought the Donna bitch was in a state of exaltation, when you saw her running from the house.

Getting dark outside, the colour drained away, as though they'd hosed it clean, as though they'd pulled the plug and rinsed it down the sink. Joe was leaning on the bonnet, oblivious of everything, absorbed in rolling the perfect fag. He licked the paper down and stuck it in his mouth, exuding such convincing calm it was almost catatonic. The briefest flame, an orange glow of inhalation, and a half-burnt match was tossed away.

But it doesn't take long to run down a drive. Even in your three-inch heels, when you're not the sporty type, and it's a longer sort of drive in a better part of London, you can cross it fairly quickly. The gravel tends to suck you down, but you can manage, if you concentrate. And as she tottered forward, her breath condensing in the air, her underrated Donna brain began throbbing in her head, quietly pulsing beneath the bone, for she's thinking of that ever-grinning piece of pus who answers to the name of Merv. Fifteen seconds to climb the stairs, another five to walk down the hall, then he'd step inside the fatman's den, and . . .

'Joe!' she shrieked. 'We're going, Joe!'

You had to hand it to the boy, he could shift himself when he really had to. He was round the front and in the seat before she'd caught her breath, before she'd finished sucking air. He leaned across, shoved open the door, and she slipped inside.

'You OK?'

'Yeah, I'm OK. Are you OK?'

'I'm fine.'

I wiped your debt, she nearly added, got a bonus, too. She'd stuffed it in her bag, she'd crammed it in and snapped it shut. Safe within her leather bag she had the fatman's money, the only thing of his she wanted buried deep inside. It made her panties moisten, frankly. Made her start to lubricate. All that money, on her lap, it made her melt between her legs. Because she likes it when they give her things, she loves it when they spend a bit, but she adores it when she takes it, for that's the kind of girl she is.

For they're forgetful types, the three-legs. They forget to take her out, forget to buy her what she wants, forget her name, forget the way she likes it. But they always remember to stick it in, they're always ready to push it in, they never forget to shove it in. So they owe her, really, the way she sees it. In her Donna-centric world-view, they owe her in abundance.

'We off, Joe, are we?'

'We're going, babe.'

He turned up his collar and put on his shades, for he liked to act the part, he liked to get in character. She blew on her fingers.

'So we're splitting, yeah?'

A final drag, and he chucked the roll-up out of the window.

'We're on our way.'

He turned the key. The engine coughed and spluttered out.

'Right,' he said, and tried again. The motor almost caught. It very nearly almost fired. Three endless seconds in which it almost sparked, then quietly died. He pumped the throttle.

'You're flooding the engine.'

'You know about cars?'

'You're flooding it, Joe.'

He tried a third time. One turn to the right, and ignition on. A half-turn further, and the motor turned over, and then the tubercular sound you get, that sick, familiar, wheezing sound, when the battery starts to fade.

A spasm shook the Donna gut.

'We off now, Joe?'

'We're up and running.'

'So we're going, are we?'

'In a *minute*, OK?'

She twisted in her seat and stared back at the house. Lights were coming on upstairs, shadows moving behind the curtains. Henry's face appeared, a blob of livid malice, framed in the second-floor window. His mouth kept changing shape, for he was shouting something, expressing himself in his favoured way. She watched the hole as it opened and closed. Imagined the insults spewing forth, the globs of Henry spittle arcing through the air before landing, with a soft and glutinous hiss, on the window pane.

'No need to rush, but I think he's watching.'

'How's he looking?'

'Not too happy.'

Joe worked the motor.

'We better shift then.'

She kept her eyes on the fatman's face and moved her fingers in mute farewell.

'Yeah,' she said. 'We better had.'

Merv and Billy beside him now, and he's pointing down, giving his orders, the black-hole aperture growing and shrinking. Like watching a silent film, she thought, and suddenly realized the boys had gone, they'd disappeared, they'd scooped up their testosterone and vanished. There was just the fatman, alone in the window. And she couldn't be sure, she couldn't be certain, but it looked like he was grinning.

'Will you start the car?'

'I'm trying, aren't I?'

'Fucking start it, will you?'

'You swearing, now?'

'Just press it down. Don't pump it, right? Press the pedal *down.*'

'I been *doing* that, sweetheart.'

'Well this time, fucking *keep* it down!'

The front door burst open, like a bad, bad dream. Mervyn boiled out of the house, a six-inch length of metal pipe protruding from his fist. She thumbed down the door-lock. Joe put the gear-stick into second and floored the throttle. Mervyn running up the drive, skinhead Billy close behind. A sudden vision of being dragged upstairs, being bent and spread, abased before the fatman. Vomit-panic in her belly. Not that, she thought. Not me, she thought.

'God . . .' she moaned.

He jerked the key, the engine turned over. Then he lifted his foot, he was doing it right, and the sweet, sweet sound of a borrowed motor when it finally starts to fire. He released the clutch and the car shot forward, rear wheels spinning till they found the ground. The seductive smell of burning rubber, and Merv and Billy almost had her, they were almost touching, they were almost there.

Then the car went skidding towards the road, slamming her back against the leather seat. Like when a plane takes off, so good it was, all speed and light and potency. The fatman booty in her lap, and Mervyn screaming just behind, and adrenalin coursing through her veins.

'Joe,' she breathed, 'we're in the movies, Joe . . .'

And he gunned the engine, and they were out of there.

8

Once they'd cleared Heath Drive he cut the speed. He might not know how to start a car, but he knew about stuff like that. You keep your right foot light on the pedal, you don't go shooting off up Redington Road, panicking all the decent folk. Be like having a sign on the back of your car. Phone in my number, cause I'm a robber. It's things like that that he knows about, being quite a knowing guy. So having cleared Heath Drive he cut the speed, then just cruised along, went sailing along. Nice and slowly, sweet and easy, like he did it every night.

He palmed the gear-stick into fourth. Cold air was blasting from the vents, droplets forming inside the windows. He switched on the heater, listened to the fan. And then he asked, apropos of nothing much:

'How much you get, then?'

She didn't react. You might even have thought that the girl hadn't heard. She merely said . . .

'We eating soon?'

. . . and turned her head to look at him. He was a good-looking boy, and she liked to look. There was stubble on his cheek, for he didn't care to shave too much. Just now and then, when he got the urge. He said he'd do it, if she wanted, but she told him not to bother, for she likes her men to look like blokes, she likes them post-pubescent.

He hung a right into Arkwright Road.

'You hungry, babe?'

'Well . . . not exactly.'

'But you wouldn't say no?'

'Might pass the time.'

'So how much you get, then?'

Because he hadn't forgotten.

'Get, Joe?'

'Get, babe. Off of Henry.'

'What makes you think—'

'I can smell it, can't I. You got that money smell.'

He was coasting down, engine in neutral.

'I'm interested, that's all. I mean it's no big deal.'

She frowned at the dashboard.

'You just want to know . . .'

'I'm a curious bloke.'

'And it's finders keepers. Right, Joe?'

'Right.'

She wrapped her arms around the bag and clutched it to her belly.

'I got plenty, Joey.'

She nodded to herself.

'I'm loaded, see.'

He slipped into first.

'What you probably mean . . .'

He went sharp left.

'. . . is that *we're* loaded, sweetheart.'

She watched the buildings go floating by and drew a large D on the misted-up glass.

'Yeah,' she muttered. 'Probably.'

Stuck in the queue at the lights by the station. Six lanes of traffic, their engines revving. Noise and filth and aggravation, the eternal stink of the Finchley Road. He adjusted the mirror, rooted for a fag.

'So how'd it go, then?'

She touched a filling with her tongue.

'All right, I guess.'

'No problems . . . ?'

'Not really.'

He crushed an empty pack in his fist and chucked it in the back.

'Did you wipe my debt?'

'I sort of wiped it.' She watched a lad on a mountain bike go threading between the cars. 'I also wiped your job.'

'Never liked that job.'

'Say thank you, then.'

'Thank you, then.'

The lights went to orange.

'You see it, did you?'

'See what, Joe?'

'His thing,' he said. 'The Henry thing.'

She picked up the pack of loose tobacco and pulled out a generous pinch.

'Might have caught a glimpse.'

He released the handbrake.

'I've seen it too,' he said. 'Such as it is.'

He was holding the clutch at biting point.

'Bit small, I thought.'

'Minute,' she agreed. She wrinkled her nose in pained distaste. To think of what he'd wanted her to do. The cheek of it. The total fucking nerve.

'Made me stop in Holland Park,' Joe said. 'Had to take a leak.'

'Right in the park?'

'In Addison Road.'

'That's Shepherd's Bush.'

'You the A to Z?'

She peeled off a paper and started rolling him a fag.

'So you stopped the car . . .'

'And he had the leak. Did it in the porch of this redbrick place. Right in the porch, right on the door.'

She shook her head.

'Not nice, that, is it.'

Joe nodded sadly.

'Quite nasty, really.'

The line of traffic began surging forward. He took a right, and they sped through Kilburn. Then Kensal Green, the Scrubs Lane junction, and before too long they were hitting Harlesden, with its corrugated lock-ups and quick deals for cash, no questions asked.

'You done my fag, yet?'

'I'm doing it, Joe.'

He pulled off the high street and looped round the houses, riding the brake so he could check the numbers. Night had fallen, and he dispensed with the image and took off his shades. She looked up from the ciggy, stared out through the tinted windows. There weren't a lot of cafés, really. Not a lot of nightlife.

'We stopping here, are we?'

'Just taking a spin,' he said. 'Just passing through.'

'And then we have our dinner, yeah?'

'Soon, babe,' he said. 'Few minutes, OK?'

He drove up onto the pavement, beside an eight-foot, fly-postered wall.

'Have to do some business first.'

'What kind of business?'

'Motor business, precious. Not your thing, I would have thought.'

She licked down the paper and passed him the roll-up.

'You dumping the car, then?'

He cut the motor.

'It's got to go.'

'I like this car.'

'We can't all get the things we like.'

She pulled down the vanity mirror and moistened her lips.

'I think you get plenty, Joe.'

'You reckon, do you?'

'Yeah, I reckon.'

The warm engine was ticking over. They smiled at each other in the deepening gloom. He got out of the car and went through a small door cut into high wooden gates. A couple of minutes later, the gates swung open and he came back out and drove them through. He circled slowly round, parking next to a stripped-down Bristol.

They climbed out and stood in the yard. Fluorescent light was shafting down, and the smell of spraypaint hung in the air. She watched the owner heave the gates shut.

'All right, is he?'

Joe sucked his lip.

'More or less.'

He'd brought them to someone he vaguely knew, a man called Phil, a friend of a nodding acquaintance. A lanky, thin-haired man with bloodshot eyes and a runny nose. There was an Austin-Healey parked near by, and a Mercedes hard-top round the back, because Phil was quality, only dealt in the best. They watched him wipe his hands on his overalls and stroll towards them, barely glancing at their motor. A brief nod to Joe, and he took the matchstick out of his mouth.

'How much?'

Joe looked him in the eye.

'It's worth over thirty.'

'I know what it's worth,' Phil said. 'Give me a figure.'

'Twenty.'

The man's face creased into a smile.

'Three,' he said softly.

'Do me a favour . . .'

'I'm trying to.'

Dust was shimmering in the artificial light.

'Fifteen,' Joe muttered.

The man wiped his nose with the back of his hand.

'You're not really in a strong position,' he said. 'Not really,' he said. 'Not for bargaining, if you get my drift.'

'It's a bit hot, that's all.'

'It's scorching, my son.'

'Twelve, then.'

'Three and a half,' Phil said. 'And I'm being generous.'

The man shoved the matchstick back in his mouth.

'Done?'

For a moment, Joe hesitated. He scuffed the toe of his shoe against the tarmacked ground and seemed to shake his head. And then his body sagged, his whole frame drooped. It was as if he'd been shoved against a wall, as if they'd pinned him by the arms and punched him in the solar plexus.

'Done,' he muttered.

They waited out in the yard while Phil disappeared into a prefab shed to get the cash. She was beginning to feel vaguely bereft. No more trips in Henry's car. No tender Donna rump on the shiny leather seats.

'Never mind,' she soothed. 'It's only money.'

(The most mindless thing she'd said in at least three hours.)

Phil came out again after a couple of minutes and walked towards them. He was tossing a set of keys from one hand to the other.

'Fancy a new motor?'

'I'd like that one,' she announced, pointing at the Austin-Healey.

Joe grinned and punched the man lightly on the shoulder.

'Don't go winding up my lady.'

Phil grinned back at him.

'Can't help it, squire.' The grin went stiff. 'But you need some wheels, right?'

'Might do.'

'I mean you need them bad, right?'

'You making an offer?'

The man fiddled with his nose again.

'Just a suggestion.'

'So what you got, then?'

'Mark Two Capri.'

Joey nodded, thinking it over.

'Runner, is it?'

'Like a rocket. It's a wide-boy motor, if you know what I mean.'

He led them round to the back of the shed and there it was, in shades of blue: a two-tone Ford Capri. Joe lifted the bonnet and peered at the engine.

'Bit clean,' he muttered.

'It's for the punters. You know they're fussy.'

Joe started walking slowly round, kicking the tyres, running his fingers over the body. He squatted down in front of the radiator and squinted along the wing.

'Got a new door,' he noted.

Phil chewed the matchstick.

'I'm not saying it hasn't had work.'

Joe hauled himself to his feet.

'Can we get it on the ramp?'

'Bit late for that. Have to think of the neighbours.'

'Yeah,' Joe grunted. 'Sure.'

He glanced at Donna and raised his eyebrows. She shrugged and nodded.

'I'll give you eight hundred,' he said.

Phil snorted. He pulled out the rod and banged the hood closed.

'You don't get it, do you?'

'Get what?'

'Punters like you get special prices.'

'A grand,' Joe said, 'and we drive away.'

'Three and a half,' Phil countered, 'and I'll fill the tank.'

Joe gazed at him.

'You know what you are?'

'I'm a dealer, son.'

'You're a nine-carat cunt.'

Phil shrugged.

'Same thing.'

9

'We could always go abroad,' she said.

It was only a suggestion, her way of being helpful, her Donna contribution for the evening. They'd found a room in Finsbury, a quite appalling room, but she'd blocked it out, she's not complaining. Small double bed, an unshaded bulb, and it's twenty-three pounds, all charges included. There wasn't a telly, though you had your own shower. But it's got a smell, and she knows that smell, a syrupy compound of damp and decay, like a place she'd stayed in Camden. For Donna's been around a bit, been shifting herself around.

'Just shoot off abroad, just the two of us.'

She looked at herself in the mirror.

'Be quite romantic. Like a honeymoon.'

'You mean somewhere foreign?'

'Somewhere like that.'

She put a finger on the shadowed skin beneath her eyes and pulled it gently down. Inflamed, she thought. I'm dying.

'Where they do pasta,' she added.

'I don't like pasta.'

'Where they do burgers, then.'

He was lying on the bed, staring up at the ceiling. He had his shoes on, which bothered her, but only slightly. She leaned towards the glass and scrutinized her reflection. A small, pink lump had formed on her chin.

'I've got a spot, Joe.'

'I know.'

'Maybe it's a guilt spot, because I took an old man's money.' She peered closer.

'My conscience must be troubling me.'

'You haven't got a conscience,' he murmured. 'You've got a spot.'

'Do you think that bloke downstairs noticed?'

'I think he did.'

'Is it very noticeable?'

'What do you want me to say?'

'Say no.'

'No.'

'I'll put some stuff on it tomorrow.'

'Why don't you just squeeze it?'

'Makes them spread, if you do that.'

'They're spreading already.'

'That supposed to mean something, is it?'

'It means you had one the other night.'

'Which night?'

'The night we met,' he said. 'Round at Carlo's.'

'That was a period spot.'

'A what spot?'

'*You* remember, sweetie: off our food, and blood everywhere . . . ?'

'Oh yeah.' He rolled over onto his side. 'I remember.'

It had been gone eleven when they got there. A bed-and-breakfast cheap hotel, the sort of place you hate on sight because it strips away the fantasy and reminds you that you're poor. They'd had to pay upfront, so they booked themselves in for just a couple of nights. Forty-six pounds, plus fifty on top in case of breakages. Everything costing, everything dear.

When the guy in reception handed over the keys, he'd had that look on his face, that caretaker's smirk. She saw it in his eyes, a 'hello, darling' type of look, as though she were a working girl, some piece of painted flesh that rents it by the hour. She'd had a sudden urge to tell him who she was, to let him know the things she'd done, that she and she alone had been the one to rob the fatman. Instead of which, she held her peace. Just followed Joe upstairs, and stepped inside the room, and peeled off the skin-tight jeans and talked to him of spots and pasta.

She crossed to the table and picked up a ciggy, sliding it smoothly between her lips. There was a soft grunt as he heaved himself off the bed, a muted exhalation as Joey made an effort. He struck a match and held the flame a few inches in front of her face. She leaned forward and sucked heat into the weed. Nothing like it, she was thinking, for it's her all-time, second-favourite sensation. She took a long and perfect drag and held the smoke inside her lungs, almost beyond the limit, until it seemed the lungs would burst.

'You shouldn't do that,' he said.

'Do what?'

'That smoke thing.'

He shoved the matches back in his pocket.

'One day you'll go too far.'

'I know.'

'One day you'll die.'

'I know.'

Her bag lay on the bed. She pulled him down beside her, shoved a hand inside, and took out the wad of currency. And the Donna bitch can't help it, but just holding it, just gripping Henry's money in her hot and eager fingers, makes her quietly start to lubricate.

'Looks a fair amount,' he said.

She nodded.

'Yeah. Done well here, Joe. Going to live in style.'

She spread it all out on the nylon quilt, and almost ached with adoration. Crisp, new notes, unfingered by humanity. Unsullied bits of paper they could use to run away. All mine, she thought. She glanced across. All ours, she added.

He flexed his fingers.

'You want to count it?'

She shook her head.

'I took it, Joe. You count it.'

He leaned forward and collected several tens into a small pile.

'That's a hundred,' he said.

'Good start,' she said.

'There's heaps more,' he said.

'Loads,' she agreed.

It didn't take long to add it up, but they still checked twice, just to be sure. Four hundred pounds, which is not a lot to take, not too much to liberate. Not when you're the Donna bitch, and you like the feeling of silk against your skin. Four hundred quid off a millionaire. It's nothing, frankly. Fuck all, if you're counting. Four hundred lousy quid to start a life.

Better not take a sum like that. When you rob a man like

Henry, you'd better take it all, or leave him be. You shouldn't dip your fingers in his pocket and steal a bit to tide you over. You should take the bread from his mouth and the clothes off his back, and leave him naked in the street, alone and helpless in the street. Just take it all, or leave him be.

For there's one thing Donna ought to learn: never provoke a rich man, because rich men take revenge. So when she slipped the notes inside her bag and left him dripping on the floor, she was being soft, too tender-hearted, letting charity prevail. Should have flogged his things and burnt the house, just torched it to the ground.

The bastard would have understood. Might not have liked it, but he'd have understood. Some poor, mad bitch who comes in from the cold and looks around with hungry eyes. They half-expect it, men like him, for it's what their nightmares are made of. And when they wake up sweating in the night, they've been dreaming of girlies like Donna.

She gathered up the tens and twenties.

'I mean you don't like abroad, anyway,' she said, 'I mean, do you, Joe?'

Stacked them together in a small, neat pile.

''Cause East, West – home's best. That's what they say, see?'

He nodded.

'I guess.' He shrugged. 'But mustn't grumble, eh, babe? Keep on smiling, right?'

'Yeah, Joe. Sure.'

For she knows they're losers, him and her. Just punters, really. The sort of kids who get screwed a lot. They've got it written on their foreheads: I am nothing, on this earth. They touch a diamond and it turns to dust, for as Henry would have put it, as the fatman might have said, it's their true and only destiny to live a shitty life.

She's always known she'll lose. It's in her blood, inside her bones, this recognition that she's something less, she'll never bridge the gap, she'll never reach the other side. And Joey-boy, her man of choice, is a poor, soft lad. Been born like that, and he'd stay like that. For he didn't understand, it hadn't yet impinged upon his throbbing Joey brain, that he'd been robbed before he'd even started, crushed before he had a chance. They'd stolen his life before it began, and all he could do was to pull on a mask, take out a cosh, and do his best to steal it back.

But Joey was devoid of rage. That was one of Joey's troubles. Even when they kept him down, had their foot on his face and his face on the ground, he never hungered to finish them off, just wipe them out, just blow a neat, round hole in the back of their heads and slowly walk away.

So that was Joe. Big, stupid guy. Called him Joey, to show how much they liked him, the way they'd like a dog. They'd slipped a collar round his neck, clipped on the leash, and led him round, their Joey-boy. Kept him down on all fours, his tongue hanging out and his tail tucked away.

She sighed to herself as she got undressed. Didn't say anything, because there's nothing to say. Just folded her clothes and stowed them away. A five-minute shower with lukewarm water, then in the bed and move up close. The touch of skin on tender skin, the almost copulation.

Because they might be losers, him and her, they might be nothing, on this earth, but mustn't grumble, keep on smiling.

That right, Joey? Eh, Joe? Eh?

10

A half-remembered sound seeped in from the corridor and forced her awake. She opened her eyes in the dark. The smell of the room billowed over her, everything seedy and everything soiled.

She couldn't fuck, in a room like that. Couldn't spread herself and let her boy inside in a twenty-pound room in Finsbury. For that is one of Donna's problems, this is one of her neuroses, that she can't just do it anywhere. She can't start rutting, in a place like that, can't lubricate beneath a greasy blanket, can't let the boy amuse himself when bugs might plummet from the ceiling, when there's grime embedded in the carpet, and some nameless slime beneath the bed. She starts imagining the germs inside the pillowcase, the insects crawling in the sink, the dust mites breeding in the wardrobe. She can't help it, really, for it's how she thinks, and she's always been quite thoughtfully inclined.

Her fantasy, the major Donna wish she'd like to see fulfilled, is a first-floor flat in a stucco-fronted house, the decoration minimal, all empty space and polished floors, without the detritus of other people's lives piled up around, their pustular belongings squatting on the carpet. Instead of which, instead of being someone of significance, she's lying on a bed a vagabond would burn, in a dismally ungenerous room that reeks of takeaways and urine.

That sound again, that urgent whisper, just outside. A smothered laugh, high-pitched and slightly female. And suddenly, the beating Donna heart, the vomit-panic churning in her belly, the consciousness of Joe asleep beside her.

Outside in the passage, someone pursed his lips and softly blew, and a spurt of skinhead breath came jetting from his mouth.

'Psssst!'

It's strange when you can hear someone grinning in the dark. When you listen to the air as it's forced between his teeth, and you know he's standing outside, with his hand on his crotch, and he's grinning, quite benignly, in the dark.

Laughter bubbled in the corridor and a steel-toed boot thudded into the door. There was a sudden, whiplash crack as the lock began to give. So loud it was, you could have heard it miles away, could well have heard it in Redington Road, if you'd been listening hard enough. The footsteps moved away, and she clutched the blanket, allowed herself to half-believe they'd gone, then heard the feet come running back, heard them pounding up the passageway, and the floor shook beneath the bed, it trembled underneath, as something heavy slammed against the door.

It's never happened, a thing like this. This is something new for her, a first in her eventful life, and it takes a while to comprehend. For although she took a rich man's cash, and ran off with a boy called Joe, and should have had the sense to know what might transpire, it takes a while to recognize that her shabby little world, pathetic as it is, is about to be invaded.

The middle panel sagged, caved in, split apart. A gloved fist appeared in the gap. Like that film, she told herself. Joe, she thought, we're in the movies, Joe. She couldn't breathe. She knew she ought to, but she found she couldn't. They'd stolen all the air, they'd sucked away the warm, damp air. She moved her lips. High-pitched sounds inside her head, little whimpers of disbelief. That's me, she thought, that's Donna bitch. There was an endless splintering of cheap wood and chipboard, and the hinges abruptly gave. The door buckled and swung open. The boys erupted into the room.

The ceiling lamp flicked on. A moment of sweet silence.

Billy scratched his cheek.

'Hello, scumbags.'

The vomit-panic churning in your gut, because you're only a soft-boned girly, and you didn't mean to cause offence, and now they're through the door and standing by the bed, they're standing smiling by the bed.

Mervyn's sweet, cherubic face.

'Thought we'd just pop in,' he said. 'Seemed the decent thing to do,' he added. 'As we were passing, so to speak.'

He was holding a cream-coloured baseball bat. There was a red stripe painted round the tip. About two a.m., it must have been, that dead and buried time of night when no-one hears, when every sound is muffled. The skinhead frowned.

'Think we've disturbed them, Merv?'

'I think we have, Billy. I think the fuckers were fast asleep.'

'So we woke them up.'

'Looks like we did. I feel bad about that.'

'Don't feel bad, Merv.'

'No?'

'No.'

Billy reached inside his Crombie coat and pulled out something chrome and black. He pressed a button, and a blade shot out.

'Do you think they are, though?'

'Are what, Billy?'

The skinhead ran his thumb along the blade and a drop of blood, a perfect crimson sphere, began forming on the skin.

'Fuckers, Merv.'

Mervyn thought about it.

'Good question, Billy.'

'Thank you, Mervyn.'

'Because I think we should be told.'

'We should.'

'Maybe we can ask them later. Once we've done the business, as it were, we can ask them if they fuck a lot.'

'And they can tell us,' Billy said.

'Or even show us.'

'And we can watch, and make suggestions from the floor.'

'Be like sitting in the theatre.'

'I'm very partial to a bit of theatre.'

'I thought you might be.'

And they smiled at each other, for they were happy boys.

'Better start, then,' Billy murmured. 'No point waiting, as we're here.'

He came round the bed to Joey's side. He had the flick-knife in his hand, and was looking quite good, he was looking quite smart, if one's being quite honest. He'd taken pains, he'd made an effort: red Doc Martens and a velvet bow tie, for he liked to dress up, when occasion demanded. But you wouldn't want to be in Joey's place, not at that moment. Not if you've got sensibilities, which many people have. If you were lying there, with girly by your side, you might have felt a sudden, burning pain, a spasm in your bladder, as you watched the wordless Billy gazing down.

The skinhead sighed, and shook his head. You could almost see what he was thinking. He was thinking: Hello, mate. It's a funny old world. And more in sorrow than in anger, he placed a knee on the naked chest, and leaned his full weight forward. Then he pressed the blade so close against Joe's neck that a breath too deep would break the skin, and said:

'Over to you then, Merv.'

Which meant: it's her turn, now.

And Mervyn said:

'It's your turn, now.'

The red-painted tip of the baseball bat. The rhythmic slapping against his palm. He could have hefted that thing above his head, could have stepped up close and braced himself. He'd pause for a moment, let her savour for a moment, then he'd bring it down, he'd swing it down, he'd slam it down upon her head. The cracking of the Donna skull. Splintered bone. Nose smashed flat against the cheek. Incandescent pain.

'Joe . . .' she whispered.

He swung the stubby end towards her.

'Like the stripe?'

Pushed it up against her mouth. Not too hard, didn't ram it in. Just pushed it gently against her mouth.

'I said d'you like my stripe?'

Does she like the stripe?

The slightest motion with her head, a nod of acquiescence, the sort of movement you tend to make when power steps inside your room with a club in its hand and a grin on its face.

'Because you should have said, see, if you liked it. Shouldn't have waited to be asked. Should have told me straight away.'

The pleasing touch of polished wood on soft and yielding mouth.

'I'm right, though, aren't I? I mean you should have *said*.'

The Mervyn frown.

'Say sorry, then.'

She mumbled something, moved her head.

'I think I missed that, darling.'

'I'm sorry, Merv.'

'Because . . . ?'

'I should have said.'

And something passed across his face, for he'd made his mark, he was getting through. So persevere, he told himself, don't stop now.

'Like the whole bat, do you? Or just the stripe?'

Pause for half a beat, to let the question percolate.

'I like all of it.'

'That the God's own truth?'

She nodded.

'Yes.'

'Cause if you like it, see, you ought to kiss it, really.'

He's holding it flat, like a red-coned torpedo.

'Am I right, there, Billy?'

'As ever, Merv.'

'So kiss it, precious . . .'

Pushing it slowly against her mouth.

'That's perfect, sweetheart. Just spread the lips, you're doing fine. Now lick it . . . yeah, all round the tip. Good girl,' he said, 'you're doing great.'

And he touched himself where he liked it best.

'She gorgeous, Billy, or is she not? Cause when you look at her, really look at her . . .'

'Please . . .' she said.

'Did she say please?'

'She did.'

'You think she means: please can I have some?'

'She does.'

'Please . . .' she whispered, for she's only a soft-boned girly, and she knows she's a loser, really. She's got it written on her forehead: I am nothing on this earth. Predestined for a shitty life.

'Look,' he said, 'be nice, why don't you. A gentle grope, with my middle finger. I've trimmed the nail, cause I empathize, so you be nice, and I'll be gentle, just a little feel for Merv the Perv, and—'

An animal noise, a blur of movement, and Joe half-flung himself on top of her. Joe, she thought, we're in the movies, Joe. And the warmth of him, the flesh on tender flesh. So when they started beating him, she could feel his ribs vibrate, she could feel it through his bones. I'll be your shield, he'd said, just you and me, he'd said, against the world. I'll swallow all your pain, he'd said, for that's the kind of man he is. No home, no hope, no money, but he'd fling himself on top of her and swallow all her pain. And when they started beating him she felt his ribs vibrate, could feel it through the bones. Then he's on the floor, and all she sees is Billy's knee moving up and down, and a flash of red Doc Martens.

A Mervyn sigh.

'Where were we, then? Oh yeah.'

And, smiling politely, he spread a hand across her mouth and slid the other between her legs. He pressed his lips against her ear and he whispered softly, murmured gently, the dulcet tones of Merv the Perv:

'Should get a nightie, darling, cause it's winter, see? You'll catch your death, if you're not careful.'

Pause for thoughtful probing down below, and he removed his hand, he eased it out.

'Sorry we can't stay long,' he said. 'Just a flying visit. Just to say hello. The bossman sends his best, by the way. Says you took something off him.' He sniffed his fingers.

'Says he wants it back.'

He pulled the quilt on top of her and carefully patted it down.

'OK, Billy?'

'Nearly finished . . .'

A final bit of self-expression, and the skinhead sauntered out.

'So anyway, darling.'

Mervyn coughed politely and straightened his cuffs.

'I'm glad we've had this conversation.'

He tucked the bat beneath his arm.

'Cause I feel we've bonded, now.'

And he gave her a cheerful, wide-boy wink and left through the broken door.

11

If she had to drive, she liked to drive at night. Orange street lamps, frost and sudden fog. Silence, speed and darkness. Black sky, no stars, and all you could see were the maladjusted lights of the oncoming cars: looming, blinding, passing.

It was four a.m. Something like that. Two short hours since the boys had been, and the noise was still inside her head, the pink and grinning double act of Merv and Billy by the bed. Her skull felt soft, as if they could have prised it open, cracked it like a rotten nut and peeled away the bone. She wrapped her fingers round the wheel. Her brain was throbbing. She was feeling bad.

'You all right?'

'Yeah I'm all right.'

She pushed open the quarter-light. Cold air cut into her face. Not long now, she thought. Few more minutes. Nearly there. She glanced at Joe. He was staring straight ahead, the street light flickering across his cheek. There was a scab of blood on his lower lip, a purple bruise along the swollen jaw. Him and her, she told herself. Less than nothing. Minus nothing. She felt the steady beat inside her head, the pulse of recognition, as if her brain might suddenly become engorged, explode with comprehension. Him and her, she told herself. The shit on Henry's shoes.

She changed down to second, went powering through an amber light, and they're speeding past the Heath. Mellow, redbrick houses. Gravelled drives. Discreet and tree-filled gardens. The wealth so lightly worn: a modest Turner here, a Canaletto there. Hampstead Town in all its glory. A bit of posh, to which one might aspire.

She managed not to look, stayed focused on the tarmac. Foot down hard and she's scudding down the road, shooting past the affluence. But still the wind came rushing through the trees, the collective sigh, the shared and sanguine exhalation, of sleeping Hampstead folk. Look at us, it whispered. Feast your eyes on plenitude. See how we live, and marvel. Worship how we live, you bitch.

'You like this place?'

He was speaking softly as he looked out the window.

'Not bad,' she said.

'Because the boys don't like it.'

He wiped some moisture from the sweating glass.

'They don't like folk who can pay their way. Seems to wind them up a bit. Gives them aggravation.'

He watched the trees go coasting past.

'But they come round Kilburn, and they're laughing. I mean you put them in some rubbish-place, and what you've got is happy boys. They know where they are in a shithole, see. So when they come round my place, they come in grinning.'

You could almost hear it, the Joey brain, kicking into gear.

For the scales were falling from his eyes, the doors of perception were inching open. Because the Joeys of this earth, they go through life and there's nothing that offends them, nothing seems to drive them wild. Nothing makes them want to pull a half-brick from a wall, and wrap it in a woollen sock, and go out in the night and search for meaning in their lives.

They never get the urge to desecrate the sanctum. They accept existence as it is, and swallow what they're given. They eat a little piece each day, a piece of excrement each day, a freshly fallen, newly minted, moist and steaming turd each day, then lick their lips and ask for more. And Joe's beginning, just beginning, to find the taste repellent.

'They entered our room,' he said.

'I know.'

'Our private place.'

'I know.'

He stared into the darkness.

'He touched you, did he?'

She waited a moment. Better don't rush, she told herself. Think, for once, before you answer.

'Only with the bat,' she said. 'Against my mouth.'

Joe listened politely.

'With his finger,' he suggested. 'Between your legs.'

She shook her head.

'He didn't.'

'I thought he did.'

'It just looked like it.'

He shaped his lips and blew warm air onto the glass, which gradually started to mist up again.

'But did it feel like it?'

'No.'

Joe rubbed his jaw.

'So he didn't.'

She changed down to second.

'Only on my thigh,' she said.

'So he did.'

'Not where it mattered.'

'So he didn't . . .'

She turned into the narrow, wooded roads of the village.

'He didn't.'

Noise and movement in her head, and the Mervyn thing came flooding back. Good girl, he'd said. That vacant, bovine, sodden face. Behave, he'd said, and pressed the wooden bat against her mouth. And then the finger shoved below, the middle finger, with the nail he trimmed especially. Thick and moist, like a garden worm. Made her want to gag, to think of it. Made the bile begin to rise inside her throat. So block it out, just block it out. Foot down hard, lights on main beam. Let's go for a drive, she'd said. Let's take a spin, why don't we. So here they were, just her and him, about to pay a call. The worm between her legs. Never happened. Just block it out.

She took a left into Redington Road, the *déjà vu* of Redington Road. The dull, metal gleam of parked limousines, the cautioning hum of near-silent alarms, and above it all, hovering somewhere in the Hampstead air, the dense, un-troubled hush, the deep and trusting exhalations, of the sleeping bourgeoisie. For it's that raw and jagged hour, that sweet and fetid time of night when all is quiet, and nothing stirs, and decent folk are in their beds.

She let the motor crawl along. No hurry, now. Just take it slowly, nice and easy. Into first and inch along. Scan the road, and there it was, twenty yards down on the right-hand side, behind a brick wall and through a locked gate. The fatman's mansion. Squatting, like a half-wit, in the dark. She felt a brief and fleeting satisfaction, that sudden, heady feeling you get when you've been driving through a frozen night and you finally arrive. She nudged the car against the kerb and cut the lights.

A video camera peered down from the corner of the porch. There were bars and grilles on the windows, movement sensors and panic buttons. And that locked and bolted door, the slab of steel behind the oak facade, for the fatman wasn't stupid, he might have been vulgar, but he wasn't stupid. He'd built a castle against the mob, in case the mob should get ideas. Let the riff-raff putrefy. Let them rot inside their stinking homes. Let them bash each other on the head and steal each other's benefit, for Henry couldn't give a toss. He's tucked up safely in his bed, fast asleep and snoring hard, his limp and flaccid Henry cock glistening on his thigh.

She switched off the engine.

'Here we are, then.'

He shifted his weight on the seat.

'Yeah.'

She listened to the silence. A special kind of silence. It hung low above the rooftops and crept inside the car. Curled around her head and made her think of happy times.

'I saw this policeman once,' she said. 'Down Kensington.'

She wrapped the scarf around her neck.

'A nice young bloke, all navy blue and cleanliness.'

'Could you marry one?'

'A copper, you mean?'

'Get a bloody good pension.'

'I'd think about it. So anyway, he's walking past some big, flash car – which is on a double yellow – and he sort of stops,' she said, 'and scrapes it.'

'Like Billy, when he's in a mood.'

'Just scraped the paintwork, with his key.'

'What about the driver?'

'Wasn't there,' she said.

She pulled the quarter-light shut.

'No-one's there. Just me and him.'

Winter rain began spattering on the roof.

'And as we're about to pass each other, he gives me this glance from under his helmet, and there's this look on his face, this copper smile.'

'I know that smile.'

'If there's one thing I can't stand, he says, if there's one thing I can't bear, he says, it's a cunt in a polished Bentley.'

The cooling engine ticking softly.

'Thought I was dreaming.'

'Maybe you were.'

She shook her head and quietly grinned, for just thinking about it gave her pleasure, just remembering the day was giving her glee. She can't help it really, for she's that kind of girl.

'I ran my finger along the wing. Just to be sure, see. Just to be certain.'

'And he'd scraped it off . . . ?'

'Down to the metal.'

Joe whistled softly. Disturbing thoughts began flitting through his head, images of random spite and uniformed malevolence.

'If they were all like that . . .'

'Be chaos, wouldn't it.'

'Bedlam,' he muttered.

He zipped up his jacket.

'I reckon that bloke was out of order.'

'You reckon, do you?'

'Yeah, I reckon.'

He stared through the gates and turned up his collar. Acting the part, always in character.

'We going in, then?'

He was gazing at the fatman's motor. It was hugging the drive, half in shadow.

'Cause if we're going, we ought to go.'

When she stepped out of the car, the cold was so bad it seemed to burn her skin. She shoved her hands deep down in the pockets, her fingers stiffening inside the gloves. She watched him open the boot and root inside, then bring out something bulky. A muffled Joey gasp as the thing was lifted out. She cocked her head and stared at it: a foot-long wooden handle, with a cast-iron, oblong knob at the end, like something you'd use to tenderize meat.

'That for me, is it?'

He passed it across.

'It's heavy,' he muttered.

He bent and hauled out a rectangular box, laying it carefully on the ground, then pressed the boot down and clicked it shut.

'Battery first?' she asked.

'Battery's always last,' he said. 'You're the meat and two veg, I'm the after-dinner mint.'

She thought about this.

'I want to be the mint, Joe.'

'We'll see, OK?'

He took out his key and unlocked the gate. He pushed it open and they walked inside. It was one of those London nights you dream of, sharp and moonless, perfect for low-life. An ideal night for hungry types, for tooling up and dropping by, for visiting your friends before they come and visit you. A night light glowed dimly on the wall as they approached the dew-topped limousine.

She could almost smell the walnut dash, the thick-pile carpet, the hand-stitched hide on which the fatman placed his fatman rump. She sniffed a little deeper. It was a concentrated money smell, redolent of everything she'd never had and would never get, and she felt a tiny stab of pain, a fleeting sense of deprivation, an orange flame of rage, a consciousness of being outside looking in. Donna, with her face pressed up against the window, with her damp and anxious longings, with the iron mallet in her hand. The Donna bitch. The sweet, uncaring, soft and yielding, pain-avenging Donna bitch.

For this was him, their lord and fucking master: a piece of filth in a velvet jacket, a gibbering ape in a chauffeured car. She touched the coachwork with her calfskin finger. It felt smooth and thick, densely perfect.

Something gleamed in Joey's hand.

'You ready, Joe?'

He closed his eyes for a moment and passed his hand across his face, as if to rub away the tiredness.

'Yeah.'

He cleared his throat, spat quietly on the ground.

'Nice motor, though.'

He squatted down.

'Shame we've got to . . . you know.'

He stuck the knife into an offside tyre. Grunting slightly, for they were quality tyres with inch-thick treads, and he had to shove the blade quite deep to puncture the inner tube. Stab and rip, stab and rip, all the way round. Quite physical, she thought. A very blokey thing to do. Felt slightly sick, though, when she saw it. Slashing tyres, and things like that. It was vandal stuff, toe-rag stuff, teenage-yobs-in-Fulham stuff. They were being weak, too liberal-minded, letting decency prevail. Should have gone and slashed the fatman. Should have stuck him with a Stanley knife, gouged out a thick and gristly bit and fried it with their brekker.

Joe straightened up and folded the blade.

'You doing the mallet, right?'

'Bit heavy, Joe.' She laid it on the bonnet. 'Thought I'd do the keys first.'

He dropped them into her outstretched hand.

'You got to press down hard, like your copper friend.'

'You think I can't do it?'

'I think you're delicate.'

He moved up close. She'd snagged her jeans, and there was a plum-sized hole on the back of her thigh. He pushed his finger through the gap and touched the Donna skin. The barest touch, which barely made her quiver. He drew her nearer, bent and kissed her in the dark.

But pleasure later, business first. She gently pulled away.

'Have to work now, Joe. Trash the fatman's baby.'

She stepped towards the Bentley.

'Got to press down hard?'

'You got to do it, babe.'

'Press really hard, or just press hard?'

'Press really hard.'

They'd scrape that car, she told herself, denude it of its colour. Run a key along the wing and listen to the melody. Strip off all the paint and see what's underneath. Peel back metallic silver and find the primer underneath. They'd leave their mark, she told herself. They'd leave their fucking mark.

She put the tip of the key against the metal and pressed down hard, pressed really hard, moving slowly along the wing. The key jumped, then caught, and began ploughing through the paintwork. The noise it made. Took her back a few years. Her foul, disgusting schooldays, when the chalk suddenly snapped, and the teacher scraped a fingernail on the blackboard, and all the kiddies winced and cringed. It was like that noise, but multiplied. Like that noise, but a hundredfold. In her skull, inside her brain, the noise she made on Henry's car.

'Can't do it, Joe.' She shook her head. 'I'm delicate.'

He got her something from the boot. Because he loved her, as he put it. Because he really cared. It was long and heavy, made of metal. Told her it was used for prising off the hubcaps. Like a crowbar, he explained. He stood her by the offside wing, her back to the car and a smile on her face.

'Just lift it up, then let it drop. Just swing it down. Just let it flow.'

She shut her eyes and held her breath. Easy, this, she told herself.

'Watch me, Joey.'

She raised the bar above her head.

'You watching, Joe?'

'I'm watching, babe.'

She swung it down, she let it flow. The windscreen splintered, then caved right in. It shattered into tiny shards. Like music to her dainty ears, for like many of the lower class she likes the sound of breaking glass. Could have been a yob, she realized. Could have been a ranting yob, gone running down the road with all her yobby mates.

Voices floated up the street, and a light came on next door. Joey grinning his Joey grin and pleasure coursing through her veins as a single drop of molten heat came slowly trickling out. Oh bliss, she thought. Oh ecstasy.

He squatted down beside the box and unscrewed the yellow caps. Have to shift, now. Have to hurry. A sudden whiff of chemical, which made her eyes sting and her stomach lurch. He got to his feet, began waving her back. For a moment she hesitated, but only for a moment, for she doesn't want to hurt herself, she doesn't want to splash herself, she doesn't want to let the liquid touch her skin and burn the tender Donna flesh.

He pointed at a spot two yards away and she moved obediently back, then he bent down and with a soft, unconscious grunt, hefted up the battery. A quick, complicit glance at waiting girly.

'You watching, babe?'

'I'm watching, Joe.'

And he poured the liquid onto the metal, sent it sheeting out in a smooth, wide arc. Let it swing, she thought, just let it flow. Acid splashed down on the bodywork, the waxed and perfect bodywork, and the colour hissed and burned and peeled away.

'We going, Joe?'

'We're going, babe.'

He pitched the battery through the tinted rear window. I could have done that, she told herself. Would have made my night, if I'd done that. She took out her keys, hoped the fatman was watching. Just fuck the bastard, fuck him up his greasy arse, because he shouldn't have sent them round tonight, with the baseball bats and the smart remarks. She took out her lipstick and smeared her message on the steel-blue bonnet: *Eat the Rich – Donna Bitch*.

She wrapped the scarf around her face and walked towards the Ford Capri. Henry's fault, she told herself. He'd made her, frankly. He shouldn't have smacked her in the mouth, shouldn't have been such a total cunt.

For if there's one thing she can't stand, she thought, if there's one thing she can't bear, she thought, it's a cunt in a polished Bentley.

12

A telephone box off Camden High Street, and the door swung slowly shut. Pause to light a menthol ciggy. Long, thin fingers, scarlet nails. No sleep, no food, but she's plugged in, switched on, speeding on pure adrenalin.

She punched out the number and waited. Cold in the booth, her breath condensing before her eyes. She drummed her fingers on the cradle, tilted her head and read the cards. A Japanese motorbike thundered past. Carbon monoxide, her scent of choice. She glanced out the window. Wednesday morning, and the streets were heaving.

Come on, come on . . .

Must have gone out, must have taken his motor to the breaker's yard. So wait a few seconds, give him a chance. Play the lung game to pass the time. Inhale the smoke till she almost fainted, till she nearly blacked out, till the lungs almost burst. And Joey's voice inside her brain: *You'll go too far. One day you'll die.* Joey-boy, who really cared, and she wants to tell him not to worry, she wants to tell him not to fret, for there's one thing that she knows: whatever put her in her grave, it wouldn't be tobacco.

She blew a circle in the air and listened to the ringing. He's gone, she thought, he's buggered off. Give it ten more seconds, and—

He picked up the phone. The briefest pause, then:

'Yes?'

Tension seeping through the voice.

'*Yes?*'

She pressed her mouth against the receiver. The hot, damp breath of the Donna bitch.

'Hello, sweetie.'

A dense and empty silence, and then a sigh of almost pleasure came floating down the wire.

'Well,' he murmured, 'so how's my little luscious?'

She sucked on the weed. Watched the tip glow red.

'Keeping busy.'

'Visiting friends, eh?'

'Roaming round.' She took a drag. 'Having fun.'

'Thought you might be.'

'You've been thinking, then.'

'Apparently.'

'And what have you concluded?'

'You've been naughty, sweetheart, and I think you're owed a spanking.'

You could hear it down the line, the ooze of fatman happiness.

'I'll have to teach my little girl a lesson.'

She leaned against the window pane. Winter sun came shafting through the glass. It touched her skin, caressed her face.

'You reckon you can do that, do you?'

'I know I can.'

'That's very knowing of you.'

'Cause I've worked out what your problem is . . .'

'I'm not the type of girl has problems.'

'. . . cause for all your posturing, all your attitude, what you want, all you basically want, is a good, hard screw by a man like me.'

She smiled into the phone.

'You've got a big mouth, Henry.'

The sweet, seductive memory of honey in the bathroom.

'A small dick,' she added, 'but a big mouth.'

She flicked the stub to the floor and ground it out. Mashed it into paste with her three-inch heel.

Another silence. Deeper, darker, even denser. She stared at the ceiling.

'Still there, darling?'

'I'm still here, sweetheart.'

'Because I think we ought to meet,' she said. 'That's why I'm calling, see? Thought we'd have a chat, try and thrash things out. Arrange a sort of rendezvous, why don't we.'

She pulled a slip of paper from an inside pocket.

'Around lunchtime, perhaps. Keep it civilized.'

'You want to apologize, do you?'

'Something like that.'

'Well come round whenever. Cause my door is always open, my bed is always made.'

'You saying I should come round yours again?'

'I mean fuck it, darling, you know where I *am*.'

'I think I could find it.'

'So I'll see you later.'

He tried, she thought. She'd give him that.

'I was thinking of somewhere more neutral, actually.'

'Oh yeah? Like where?'

She unfolded the paper, smoothed it carefully out. Long, thin fingers and scarlet nails. No sleep, no food, but she's plugged in, switched on, speeding on pure adrenalin. A lady-like cough as she checked the address, then she pushed her lips against the phone and said:

'Got a pen there, have you?'

13

'Shall I tell you something? Shall I, darling? Divest myself of my inner thoughts? Because I think you ought to know, you see. I think you ought to be informed.'

He was sitting beside her on the plastic bench, perspiring in his overcoat, his fleshy thigh against her knee, his sweetly rotting oldman's breath blowing lightly in her face. Half-past twelve in a West London nick, and it was giving him grief just being there. The fatman stress was thickening the air. It was billowing smoothly around their heads, lapping against the pea-green walls, dripping down the paintwork. His scalp was beginning to sweat and his guts were beginning to ache, and the Donna bitch was feeling good, for she'd made the fatman suffer.

'When I saw my car,' he said, 'when I stepped outside the door and saw my favourite car,' he said, 'the ground was shifting beneath my feet. You know what I'm saying? I'm saying my sense of order, of how the world goes round, my sense of right and wrong, my sense of *man*hood,' – liquid bubbled between his lips – 'it all was outraged. Rent asunder. Torn apart by a single visit from a single slag.'

He dabbed at his mouth with a handkerchief.

'She wants to die, I told myself. She's aching for it, isn't she. Just counting the days till we put her to sleep. Do you get my drift?'

She frowned.

'Not quite.'

He tilted his head. Hissed in her ear.

'My drift, my love, is that enough's enough.'

She half-closed her eyes to block out the glare. It made her feel ill, fluorescent light. Made her brain go soft and her face collapse, her skull begin to shrink.

'You sent the boys round, Henry. Wasn't a friendly thing to do, and I like it when you're friendly.'

Which statement cheered him up, though very slightly.

'Did it bother you, then?'

'I would have thought so, frankly. I mean Merv and Billy, all tooled up. I would have thought it bothered me. Gave me what you might call palpitations. Bit of pitter-patter in the chest. Breathlessness, that sort of thing.'

He shook his head. An indulgent smile.

'They're rascals, those two.'

'Shouldn't have done that,' she informed him. 'Middle of the night, and they're by my bed.'

'It was only business. Nothing personal.'

'But aggravating, all the same.'

'No harm intended.' He shifted his weight. 'They only wanted to have a chat. Bit of a chin-wag, if you know what I mean.'

'Well they had it, didn't they.'

'I guess they did.'

'So what's your problem?'

'It's you, my love. You're my problem of the moment. You took something from me, and I want it back.'

'Should have asked,' she said. 'That's what people do, see. They want something bad enough, they just tend to ask.'

Her gaze came to rest on the custody sergeant. He had a sallow, pasty look. Pink-rimmed eyes and narrow hips. Been eating too much prunes and custard, stuffing himself in the downstairs canteen. And a face like you get when you hate the world. He had a vicious look, when you really looked. But nice and clean, though, she reflected. Scrubbed and gleaming. You could see he washed behind the ears, which made a pleasant change. They were all like that, the lads in blue. They all looked bathed and talcumed, soaped and ready. Lean and mean and very clean.

Henry was quite clean too, she thought, considering. Because it must be hard, when you decompose, to keep the body smells at bay. But at least he made the effort. A losing struggle, possibly, but at least the old boy tried.

'Well I'm telling you now,' he said. 'Just give it back.'

'How much d'you want?'

'You trying to be clever?'

'I'm only asking.'

'All of it, darling. I want it all back.'

It was pelting down outside. You could hear it even in the lobby. Even sat inside a bomb-proof nick, you could hear the rain come sheeting down.

'I hate these places,' Henry muttered.

He had that phlegm sound in his throat, as if he'd like to hawk it clean, just spit his feelings on the floor. Just gob them out and watch them settle on the polished vinyl floor.

'Fucking loathe them.'

'Won't take long,' she soothed.

'Shouldn't have made me come here, darling.'

'Do the business, and we'll be off.'

'Full of bastard Filth.'

'Ssshhh . . .'

'Making me meet you in a cop-shop. What I'd call a vicious act.'

'At least it's warm.'

'Not a girly thing to do.'

'But fairly smart, I would have thought.'

He brought out a well-worn tobacco pouch. Squeezed it gently in his hand.

'I know,' he muttered, 'and it's why I like you. It's why I get this nice, warm feeling in my scrotum when I think of you, and I think of you a lot, these days.'

She frowned at the floor.

'Do you really, Henry?'

'Really what?'

'Get warm in the gonads . . . ?'

He smiled.

'I do.'

She let this filter through. She let it permeate her consciousness and sink into her brain.

'Tell Joey, shall I? Cause he'd like to know.'

He shook his head. The fatman grin.

'There you go again,' he said, 'just mouthing off. Like you've always got to make a noise, you've always got to wind me up. I mean normal girls, they're nice and quiet. They've got the sense to button it. Prudent, really, when you think about it. Keeping quiet, I mean, when someone's talking. Shows they've got respect, which can't be bad. But you just keep gabbing, don't you?'

She thought about this for a moment, then shrugged, and muttered:

'Yeah.'

'Such a lippy little bitch, but I'll tell you something: I like my ladies when they talk, I like it when they gab a bit. Their mouths,' he said, 'all soft and pulpy, wet and open. Quite charming, really, if you're partial. I just hold them down and pop it in, stuff their little gobs with me. Tends to shut them up, I've found. So when they talk too much, when the whining gets a touch too loud and their shrill little voices start to get on my nerves, I just bring it out and stick it in, I just pull it out and shove it in.'

A wistful look came over him.

'It quietens them, if you know what I mean. It sort of . . . calms them down.'

At which point in his dissertation, the duty sergeant glanced across and asked if he could help. Manners, she thought, approvingly, being partial to good manners. A touch of civility, here and there. Can't be bad, the way she saw it.

Henry shook his head.

'We're fine thanks, mate. Waiting for one of your D.I.'s to show.'

'Want to leave a message?'

The pink-eyed sergeant with his Mersey voice.

'We don't mind waiting.' The fatman smiled. 'We like it here.'

She watched the sergeant shrug and turn away. He had enough to do, for it was a busy station. Punters streaming in and out, and that moist, familiar, drenched-through smell that was rising from their clothes.

'You think he knows you?'

Henry shrugged.

'Might have seen me on the street, going about my lawful business.'

A wealthy sort of smirk.

'Who fucking cares, cause I don't know him.'

'He could nab you, couldn't he.'

'That scouser, you mean?'

'Put you inside.'

'Yeah', he grunted. 'In his dreams, he could. In his clammy, copper fantasies.'

She shut her eyes. Listened to the rain.

'You think you're untouchable.'

'I know so, darling.'

'Must be comforting, being you.'

'It is, my love. A comfort is how I'd put it. Because I can go down Kilburn, see a one-time hard man hobble down the road, and every step he takes, it gives him pain. And I think to myself: I did that. I made him into that. I brought him down to that. And I'll tell you something, shall I? It's the greatest feeling. Like you're flying high in the clear blue sky. Like you're the king of fucking creation.'

'Language . . .'

'Sorry.'

He began to chew his lip.

'But that's me, see? Least I try.'

'Try what?'

'Try and prove I'm still alive. That whatever I do, I don't eat shit. Not like Joe and all that garbage, namby-pamby whole-some types who lend the neighbours a helping hand, and like to do the decent thing, and have to be so fucking *nice*. Cause I just look at their smiling faces, at their shit-filled, smiling faces, and it makes me want to kill them, sometimes.'

He rolled the tobacco pouch between his fingers.

'I mean I know you prefer him, I just don't know why. Because you and me, we're what I'd term *compatible*, see. Not much to choose between us, really.'

She considered this statement for several seconds.

'There's one main difference, Henry.'

She leaned towards him and lowered her voice. She'd do her best to phrase it gently.

'One of us is a lady . . .'

The damp and fragrant Donna breath.

'. . . and the other one's a cunt.'

'Fair point,' he murmured. The glimmer of a smile. 'And elegantly put, if I may say so.'

And also true, he might have added, for the trouble with Henry was he could do what he liked. That was Henry's basic trouble. When Henry farted, everyone clapped. When he shifted his bulk on his padded seat, raised himself up an inch or two, and let the gas jet freely out, they smiled in admiration. They spread their lips and flashed their teeth to show their pleasure in the act. They sniffed the Henry-scented air, inhaled the Henry sweetness.

When Henry made a Henry joke, they laughed to show they'd got it. They delighted in his appetites, worshipped every self-indulgence. They felt in some strange way enhanced by witnessing his greed. Even when he hit them, when he slapped them round the head to emphasize his point, they tended not to mind, for power must express itself. They felt that they were privileged if he let them kiss his arse. Not just any arse, they told themselves, but *Henry's* arse.

Henry's trouble, his basic trouble, was he'd never been told the truth. No-one had told him what he really was. He'd gone through life, and no-one pointed out he was a piece of stinking filth, a glob of putrefaction in this green and pleasant land. No-one took him by the arm, and bent towards his cheek, and whispered revelations in the soft and waxy ear. They didn't hold a mirror to his face and say: examine that, you cunt. Have a butcher's, if you dare. Look at what God did to you. They never said it. Might have thought it, in their sweaty dreams, their nightly indiscretions, but not to Henry's face. Not said it, to his face.

'Shall I tell you something? Shall I? You should have done your bit, my love. Should have bowed the head, and bent the knee, and done your honest bit.'

'Couldn't help it, Henry.'

'Should have sucked me off.'

'Couldn't do it, Henry.'

'Should have wrapped your mouth around my cock and done the decent thing.'

'Had this wave, see.'

'But you left me sitting, like an ape.'

'This nausea wave, inside my gut.'

'Left me waiting, on my own.'

'This pukey feeling, deep down in my gut.'

'Left me dripping, while you ran.'

'I would have stayed. But I had to go.'

'Quite a nasty thing to do, I thought. Quite a female thing.'

'That's girlies for you.'

'I mean it wouldn't have fucking killed you.'

The fatman hiss against her ear.

'So why couldn't you, eh? You listening, darling? Why couldn't you just be nice, for once? Cause I'm only asking, aren't I. Just making conversation. So give me one good reason, you stuck-up sow.'

She thought it over for a moment, allowed herself to cogitate, and then she said:

'Thing is, Henry, you're a shade too old. A bit decrepit, as it were. Got that oldman whiff, and it doesn't wash off.'

The drooping age, that sweetly rancid odour . . .

'And I don't like to think of it, rubbing inside. Might catch something nasty, see. The slime of your collected years might leave what's termed a *residue*. Makes me feel quite queasy, frankly, and I can't help how I feel, now, can I? Can't help it, Henry, it's how I am.'

A memory of sagging flesh and brown-flecked skin.

'Not my *thing*, see, old men's cocks. I mean the *idea* isn't so bad, but the reality, sweetheart, the ghastly reality . . .'

And she shook her head, for life could be cruel.

'So that's my reason,' she concluded. 'As you asked.'

She glanced at him, but his face was blank. You couldn't tell, by watching him, what he was thinking. You had to listen hard. You had to lend an ear, and watch his mouth, and hear him say:

'You know what I'm feeling right now?'

His voice beside her, thick and gummy.

'Warm in your scrotum?'

'I feel like smashing something.'

She nodded politely.

'Better wait a bit, till we get outside.'

'Something soft and girlified.'

He was speaking calmly, very quietly.

'I could do it right now, I could finish you now.'

She watched his hands compress the pouch.

'Just snap your neck. Just wrap my hands around your neck and snap it, fairly fast.'

An understanding Donna nod.

'It's good to talk . . .'

'And the look on your face, the total fear on your slut-bitch face.'

'. . . a bit of verbal give and take, some oral intertwining.'

'Could do it, couldn't I, right here in the Filth-hole.

Thumbs on the windpipe, maintain the pressure, then that perfect sound, that whiplash crack that'll bounce off the walls. Imagine, eh? Almost feel it in my hands, the soft vibration in my hands. I could do it, darling, just finish you now . . .'

Then a sudden, high-pitched laugh, as of a fresh castrato, and he dug a finger in her ribs.

'Only joking, precious. Not an animal, am I? I mean I'd only thump you in the mouth. Right in the gob, see. Right where it hurts.'

Pause for further contemplation.

'And then I'd shove the fist inside. Try and spread your jaw and push it in. See if I could make it fit.'

A vivid image in the Donna brain: her bleeding mouth, the teeth knocked out, the searing pain as the fist goes in. They both had his fantasy in their heads, but only one of them was smiling.

She checked the clock.

'Shame we're sitting in the nick, then, isn't it? All that yearning, unreleased.'

'Almost worth it though,' he murmured. 'Almost worth a stretch inside for the look on your face, the look of surprise on your disintegrating face. I'd say that's almost worth six months or so.'

'But not quite, I reckon.'

A wistful sigh.

'Not quite,' he agreed.

There was a slow, extended hiss, and the ceiling light above their heads went out. She needs her light, she drinks it up, and it disturbed her, slightly. Not quite as much as Henry had, but slightly, all the same. She picked up her bag.

'We going to sort it, then, or we just going to sit here?'

The fatman shrugged.

'Give back the bonus and we'll call it quits. You can keep the car.'

'What about the other one?'

'The one you trashed?'

'The one we sold.'

'I've got it back.' Complacent Henry grin. 'Got a whisper from a friend, and Phil was happy to oblige.'

'So just the bonus?'

'And peace will reign. We'll be friends again.'

'No more boys . . . ?'

'Like it never happened.'

She thought it over.

'And you'll wipe the debt.'

'Can't do that, sweetheart.'

'You'll wipe it, right?'

'I'll extend his credit.'

'How long?'

'Three months.'

'Twelve.'

'Six,' he said.

'Done.'

He cleared his throat, swallowed down the phlegm.

'So call me tomorrow, right? Just dump it somewhere, and let me know. The boys can collect.'

He got to his feet.

'They like to keep busy.'

'So it's over, then?'

'It's over, sweetheart.'

He gazed at her. The bleak, grey eyes.

'Just remember, won't you: whatever you took, I'll be getting it back. Cause it's only fair, and I like to be fair. You follow me, darling? You get my drift?'

'Course I do.'

Of course she does.

With which agreement, they both shook hands. For peace will reign. And pigs might fly.

14

Joe hung a left off Lisson Grove, then left again, and pulled up by a tattered row of shops.

They'd chosen Paddington for the drop. Couldn't beat it, really. Great little place, if you like that type of thing. Perched on top of Notting Hill, and right next door to Maida Vale. Tucked in rather nicely, and always plenty of skips about. An ideal spot for dumping stuff. You just bomb along the Edgware Road until you reach the flyover, then drop your problem in a skip and quietly walk away.

You don't have to ask, because nobody cares, and even if they do, they'll very rarely mention it. They're taciturn folk in that part of town. Got that buttoned-down look on their faces, that sullen, wary, London look. That ground-down, pissed-off, fuck-you look, that makes you want to emigrate. But they're a tolerant sort, round Paddington. You can walk down the road with a cosh in your hand, and they'll move out the way if you're smiling. A very Henry kind of place, jammed with three-legs full of beer.

But you need to have an attitude, for otherwise you're shafted. If you've got no muscle, you go under. If you've got no boys to back you up, you shouldn't really step outside, shouldn't look at passers-by, shouldn't even breathe too much, if you can possibly avoid it. Better keep your head down and your voice low. Keep your window shut, and your door bolted, and hope you win the Lottery.

'I can't believe we're doing this.'

'We're doing it, babe.'

'I mean it's bad for my digestion. You hear me, Joe? This is bad for my bowels.'

'Don't say that word, OK?'

'What word?'

'You know what word.'

'You mean the bowels word?'

'Don't say it, all right?'

She shrugged.

'All right.'

He cut the engine. Silence in the car. Mid-afternoon and the sun was shining, bright and cold like a junkie's heart. Across to the right there was an endless line of greybrick flats, marching off to nowhere, while straight ahead was a patch of open space, a kind of extended yard for the local lads, where they could sniff their glue and hone their blades.

Henry territory, absolutely. Sort of place he worshipped with a passion. Somewhere he could urinate in peace. He liked to pull up in his limousine and step onto the pavement. Then he'd stride up to the wall, take it gently out, and let the goodness flow. He knew the locals wouldn't mind, being mostly in debt, mostly to him. Not for them to mind where Henry made his water. Just smile, and wave, and 'Hello Henry'. Very blokey. Nice and matey.

She wound down the window and had a look at the skips. There were two of them side by side, about thirty foot away. Dusty pink and fairly full. Aesthetically they weren't too bad. Not entirely unappealing. There was the slightest stench, if you were parked downwind, but nothing too outrageous. A vaguely dog-food kind of smell, but nothing too bizarre.

'Better do it, then.'

'You sure you don't want to?'

'It's man's work, sweetie. Rather you than me.'

For one had to be a hairy type, an uncomplaining three-leg, to shove a wodge of notes among the garbage, to poke one's hand inside the muck and leave one's benefaction. But she'd done her bit, she'd made her contribution to the cause. She'd pulled some greasy paper from a bin and wrapped it round the money-pile. It would let the fatman know she cared, let him know she valued him. Help him understand the state of her emotions.

Joe passed her a plastic carrier bag. She dropped the little package inside, rolled it up, and passed it back. He pushed open the door and gave her a look.

'Just shove it in?'

She looked at him and moved her lips.

'Nice and deep.'

He trudged off up the road. Scattered grey flakes were floating down. Not quite snow, but near enough. She watched him lower his head and hunch his shoulders and bend against the wind, too fragile for this earth. And she felt a kind of pain inside, a jagged sense of weakness, a consciousness of being helpless, of running through the city with a man who couldn't save her. A poor man, like a dead man, who would have to let her go.

Cold air gusted through the window and began to eat her skin. She shivered as she watched him. Be finished soon, she told herself. Their little escapade would finally be over. But it didn't seem right, to give it back. It left her feeling queasy. It made her want to quietly puke, to stick her fingers down her throat and feel herself regurgitate. Giving back the Henry dosh, it made her feel quite nauseous. It wasn't as if he needed it, for the Henry purse was well and truly bulging, and what he had he'd stolen. A fat and thieving man. One day she'd do it properly, she'd rob him like a Donna should: take the roof off his head, and the shirt off his back. Make him go out begging in the street. Go begging, naked, in the street.

Joe reached the skip and leaned cautiously over, peering down like it's the lucky dip. She watched him drop the stuff inside, shove it nice and deep, make it hard to find. He looked around and picked up a bin bag lying on the pavement. He slit it open, had the briefest sniff, then emptied the contents into the skip. A quick glance back and a fleeting grin. That's him, she thought. My Joey-boy.

Pink-hued street lights blinked suddenly on. He walked back to the car and climbed inside.

'All done,' he said.

'What was it like?'

'Lot of trash in there.'

'You mean builders' rubble?'

'I mean takeaways.'

He switched on the ignition.

'Lot of flies and stuff. Bit pissy, too.'

She clipped on her seat belt, for she likes to be careful.

'Good idea, then,' she remarked.

'Great idea.'

'Shame for the boys, though.'

He revved up the motor.

'Yeah,' he muttered. 'Shame.'

He drove round the block and parked a couple of streets away, then they walked back to a café nearly opposite the skip. He didn't think it was a good idea to stick around. He thought it was a fairly bad idea, in fact. Not quite as bad as robbing Henry in the first place, but pretty close. They sat one row back from the window.

'You sure you want to stay?'

'You got anything else to do?'

'They'll see us,' he said.

'They won't.'

'But they might,' he said.

'So they will.'

She sipped her tea. It was hot and sweet. Like her, she thought. Like Donna bitch. The windows were slowly misting up, but they could still see out. They'd already checked the loo, which opened onto a courtyard. Just in case, Joe had said, because you never knew when you'd have to go, you never knew when you'd have to split.

'Is that good?'

'Is what good, Joe?'

'That bacon roll.'

'Not bad.'

She took another mouthful and chewed thoughtfully.

'Not great,' she said, 'but not bad.'

He lit another cigarette.

'Do you think you might be pregnant?'

'No.'

'How d'you know?'

'Because I know.'

He sucked smoke into his lungs.

'I thought you might be, that's all.'

'Oh really?'

'Because you seem to eat . . . I mean you seem to have to eat, sort of . . . *frequently*.'

She took another bite of lettuce and streaky bacon, a taste of heaven in a sesame bun.

'You saying I eat too much? That what you're telling me?'

'Course I'm not.'

'Cause that's what it sounds like.'

'Just been wondering where it goes, that's all.'

'Well maybe I've got a worm,' she said.

'Don't say that, please.'

She paused, mid-bite.

'Say what?' she asked.

'Worm,' he said.

'Why not?' she insisted.

'Because,' he said.

She gazed at him, entranced.

'You mean I can't say worm?'

'Correct.'

'And I can't say bowels?'

'Correct.'

The gently furrowed Donna brow.

'But what if there's a worm inside my bowels?'

He stubbed out his fag.

'You're not funny,' he said. 'You know that, don't you.'

She chewed on the roll.

'Yeah, I know that.'

She swallowed it down and wiped her lips with a paper napkin. She felt better now. A nice warm glow was spreading inside. She pulled one of his ciggies out of the pack. He hesitated, for a second, then struck a match and leaned across the table.

'Thanks,' she murmured.

'Welcome,' he grunted.

He flicked the match into the saucer, and glanced out the window.

'He's here.'

She twisted round in her seat.

'Where?'

'Coming up the road.'

And there he was, easing his way through the Paddington crowd, pushing his way through the early evening crowd. Shoving gently, shouldering softly, tunnelling a path through the uncomprehending crowd. Not long now, she thought. Soon be over now, she thought.

He was wearing his black leather jacket and pale blue jeans. The Billy uniform, the clothes of Billy choice. Probably knew that she'd be watching, probably guessed that she'd be waiting. He looked scrubbed and clean and barbered, a wholesome-looking hooligan. For her, she thought. He'd shaved and primped and oiled himself for her.

He stopped a few yards back from the skip and lit a cigarette. Pause for long and thoughtful drag. That's right, Billy. Take your time. Check we're not around to jump you, do nasty things like that. Make sure you're all alone, old mate. He chucked the ciggy into the gutter. Knows he's being watched, she thought. Just knows he's being watched.

He slipped a hand inside his jacket and took out a pair of pink rubber gloves.

'He doesn't like germs.'

'He doesn't, does he.'

They watched him lean over the rim. There was a moment's hesitation as he peered inside, as if there might be something nasty down below, perhaps some piece of rotting haddock, wrapped in yesterday's *Daily Mail*. But Billy's made of sterling stuff, so he girded his loins, spat on the ground, and shoved his strong right arm inside.

Seemed to take him a while to find what he wanted. He kept bringing out cardboard boxes, and paper bags, and things that had a slimy look. His face went slowly puce, and he might have shouted something, though she couldn't be sure.

'You think he's swearing?'

'Might be, babe.'

'Pity, that. Bit vulgar, really.'

A minute or so later, the plastic bag appeared above the metal edge. Her idea, of course. Put the fatman's notes in a Mothercare bag, a girly bag for Billy-boy. And she was just beginning to indulge herself, to relish the image, to savour the moment, when all too abruptly it was over. It had barely even started, and all too suddenly it was over. She watched him walk off down the road, get in a cab, and disappear.

She sipped her tea. A sense of almost anticlimax.

So that was that then, she reflected. Gone and finished. End of story.

15

Henry stood by the window, watching a vapour trail inch across the sky. The almost-snow had gone, and it was a crisp and flawless afternoon, with sunlight shafting through the glass. He felt the tension ebb away, he felt himself begin to warm, was conscious that he mellowed in the yellow.

'Did you count it?' he said quietly.

'Yes.'

Henry narrowed his eyes against the glare, conscious of a throbbing in his gut.

'It's all there?'

'Yes.'

He turned away from the light. Billy was standing in the middle of the room. The money was on the table. Henry glanced at the clock. Three-thirty. Few more hours. Not long now. He walked over to the table and spread the banknotes out in a fan. His insides felt raw and he reached for his milk drink.

Billy judging, quietly watching. The sudden, vicious grin.

'You all right, boss?'

Henry smiled.

'I am, son.'

Spasms in his belly.

'And yourself?'

'I'm fine, boss.'

'You sure about that?'

'I'm positive.'

'So we're both all right . . .'

Henry took out his fags.

'. . . that's grand.'

The briefest hesitation, and Billy struck a match, leaned forward.

'Ta, son.'

Almost as soon as he inhaled, the fatman started coughing, hawking up mucus into a paper tissue. He held it slightly away from him, frowning at what he saw. Changing colour, fuck it. He nodded towards the hearth.

'Would you be kind enough', he said softly, 'to light that for me?'

Something unfathomable passed across Billy's face, and then he squatted down by the grate and switched on the gas, holding a match to the imitation coals. Small blue spears of flame appeared.

'Make it bigger,' Henry murmured.

The boy twisted the knob. The gas hissed louder and the flames turned yellow. He broke the match with his thumb and flicked it into the fire.

'You feeling cold, boss?'

He heaved himself up.

'You getting a chill?'

Henry stared at the boy, at his dead eyes and his scrubbed skin. The unformed teenage face, all bone and tufts and blemishes.

'You still picking them?'

'Boss?'

'Still scratching them, are you, when you shouldn't?'

'They're getting better.'

'I've got news for you.'

'Got to rub them, sometimes.'

'Oh yeah?'

'Just now and then,' the boy insisted. 'Nothing major.'

'You want to leave them alone, son, like I told you. Cause they've got germs, see? Pukey little bacteria that get under your nails. So I'd keep them under wraps, if I were you. Wear a fucking mask, or something. And keep your spotty face well out of my kitchen.'

Henry picked up the money.

'Don't go touching my food, right?'

He stubbed out his fag.

'Right?'

Billy scowled at the floor.

'Right.'

Henry shook his head. It was sad really, when he thought about it, for he gave them good advice, he tried to help, and were they grateful? Were they fuck. Who cared, anyway? It was hardly his concern what the toe-rag looked like. Long as he didn't drip pus-drops on the carpet. Long as he didn't do that. The spreading fatman smile.

'Glad I don't have to kiss you, son.'

He weighed the bundle in his hand.

'How much did you say?'

'Four hundred exactly.'

Henry nodded.

'You think that's a lot, Billy?'

'It all adds up.'

'That's very true,' the big man murmured.

He peeled off some twenties.

'And I'll tell you something, shall I? I had a lot of hassle, getting this back.'

He screwed them into a ball.

'Aggravation, one might say.'

He tossed them into the fireplace.

'And you're right,' he said, 'it all adds up.'

The skinhead watched in silence as flames began swallowing the paper. As if he couldn't quite believe, at first, that his boss was burning money.

'What you doing?' he muttered, finally.

Henry tossed in another few pounds.

'I'm baking a cake, Billy.'

The skinhead frowned.

'You being funny, boss?'

'I'm being funny, Billy.'

No sound save that of banknotes burning, and the skinhead suddenly scratching hard.

'I got filthy getting that. Went poking round in a fucking skip.'

'I know you did.' Henry's soothing voice. 'And don't think I don't appreciate it, because I don't.'

He chucked a few more notes into the flames.

'But some things are more important than money,' he explained.

Casually, as if dealing cards, he tossed the rest of the tens and twenties into the fire.

'Principle is more important, and I'm a man of principle.'

They watched the banknotes curl and blacken.

'Fuck this,' the skinhead muttered, 'I've had enough.'

Henry sighed.

'You only think you have.'

'Doing garbage for a cunt like you.'

'You too good for it?'

'I reckon.'

''Cause there's plenty more lads would be willing.'

Dismissive skinhead shrug.

'But are they able?'

Henry smiled at this, because he likes some lip.

'I've got plans for you, Billy. Things are in motion. I've got your future mapped out, and it's a great future, see, it's a shining future.'

'When do I get there, boss?'

'Give it time, son. Just do as you're told, and you'll get there. Just walk the trodden path, and you'll get to your shining future.'

Billy fingered his matches.

'But I want a shining path as well as a shining future. Feel like I'm marking time, see. Just waiting to fill a fatman's shoes.'

'Better watch your mouth there, son.'

'When you retired, I meant . . .'

'Don't get ideas, right? My boys start getting ideas, I start getting worried. So bend the knee, and shut your mouth, and walk the trodden path.'

He moved over to a rosewood bureau by the wall.

'Just come round tonight, OK? And bring the other cretin with you.'

He pulled open the middle drawer.

''Cause you know something, Billy. Shall I tell you something, eh?'

He reached inside.

'She thinks she's clever,' he said softly. 'She thinks she's really *it*.'

He took out a twelve-inch crowbar and laid it carefully on the varnished wood. Few more hours, he told himself. Not long now.

'A little girl with big ideas.'

The skinhead frowned. He looked perplexed.

'They're gone, boss . . . aren't they?'

Henry pushed the drawer gently shut. His gut felt calm, his scrotum warm.

'But not forgotten, Billy.'

16

They ate quite well, that night. They almost dined in style.
Stuffed themselves with cod and chips, were generous with the
vinegar. Pineapple fritters for the Donna bitch, and a large
pickled onion for the nice young lad. They were parked by a
chippy off Letchmore Heath. Twenty past ten, it must have
been, and the rain was pelting down. You could even hear it in
the shop, it was bucketing down so hard. Even sitting in the
corner, cramming down the fish and chips, you heard it hissing
on the empty road and running down the drain.

She was chewing on batter as the door banged open. Two
teenage lads came loping inside, all pitted skin and rampant
hormones. A fleeting recollection of her childhood days, that
damp, forgotten time of loneliness and puberty, of utter
insignificance. The endless stream of takeaways, the plate-

glass, steamed-up windows, the one-armed bandit by the wall, the sweating, moon-like face of the man behind the counter, the close-cropped lads who pushed and shoved, the noise, the stench, the wretchedness. My youth, she thought. My fucking youth.

But she's not complaining, don't get her wrong. She could have eaten that food forever. She could have swallowed chunks of fish and deep-fried chips, and washed it down with beer and cola, because she doesn't ask for much in life: wholesome grub, a fag or two, a good-looking bloke, and the fatman's money. She's a simple girl, with simple tastes. A moment's pleasure, now and then. A bit of friction, where it counts. A spot of rubbing, where she's tender, and she's happy.

'OK, that, is it?'

'It's fine,' she said.

'Not too greasy?'

'It's fine, Joe, really.'

They were leaving London, and feeling good. They'd lanced the boil of Henry's rage, and there was no more cash to burden them, no weight to press them down. They were skint again, in their natural state, the only true and natural state in which they felt at ease. The Henry problem had been resolved. It was gone and finished. End of story.

'We heading north?'

'Might as well.'

'Because I hope it's not too countrified.'

'Get away from the smoke,' he said. 'Can't be bad.'

'Because I don't like green, Joe. I'm urban, see. I like my burgers in a toasted bun, not stood in a field with flies round their eyes.'

'Just a week or two.'

He spooned some sugar into her tea.

'You'll probably like it, once we're up there.'

She gave him a suitably withering look.

'That's what you said about the jelly, Joe.'

'Was it?'

'Yeah.'

'Oh,' he said. 'Right.'

Just the bread-and-butter basics, was all they wanted. A two-room flat in a tree-lined road, a bit of cash for a good night out. Steady work and a simple life. They didn't want to take too much. They weren't too grasping, as people went. Not too demanding, as it were.

And what they didn't know, what no-one had, as yet, explained to them, was that it wouldn't be enough, to be like them. If you didn't want to take too much, and you weren't too grasping, and you didn't want to take it all, you wanted just to have the basics, it often meant you finished up with nothing.

But all that knowledge would come to them later. For now, they're sitting in a chip shop, full of warmth and happiness, and Joe drains his cup and says to her:

'Can I ask you something personal?'

She stared at him.

'How personal?'

He shrugged.

'Fairly personal.'

She took out a ciggy and let him light it.

'All right,' she muttered, 'but nothing to do with age.'

A good, long drag, to give her strength.

'I don't like age questions. Give me aggravation.'

'It's not about age.'

'So fine,' she said. 'So fire away.'

He picked up an unused fork. Scraped it along the tabletop.

'I can ask, then, can I?'

'But not about age.'

'It's not about age.'

'You can ask,' she said.

'You sure?' he queried.

'I'm sure,' she said.

'Well,' he said, 'what I've been wondering, see – and you don't have to answer this, if you don't want to – but I thought it might be interesting, and I've been meaning to mention it, the past few days. . .'

'Say it, Joe.'

'It's not about age, right?'

'Just say it, sweetie.'

'Well what I've been wondering, as you're asking, is how many men there've been.' He swallowed. 'Before me.'

The blank, unyielding Donna gaze.

'What do you mean, *been*?'

'You know . . .'

'No.'

'I mean, how many have there been?'

'Been where?'

He placed his thumb on the fork and began to spin it round.

'Been in you.'

She shifted in her seat.

'You mean right in?'

He scratched his ear lobe.

'Yeah.'

He gazed at her.

'So how many?' he said. 'Roughly,' he clarified.

She stared at his face. Such a beautiful face.

'You're the only one, Joe,' she promised. 'More or less.'

'Am I?' he murmured, taking her hand.

'Sort of,' she said.

He kissed her fingers.

'The only one?'

She smiled at him. That soft, elusive Donna smile.

'Very nearly . . .'

17

Henry picked up the saucepan and tipped it forward, and a cord of boiling milk flowed into the thermos. Wisps of steam curled out of the neck and he bent, and sniffed, and softly sighed. He stared at it thoughtfully for a moment, then added a teaspoon of honey and stirred. Because I'm nice, he told himself. Because I'm kind.

He screwed the cap back on and put the thermos near the door. He wouldn't want to forget it, in the rush. Wouldn't want to leave his milk behind and go out blindly into the night, have to do it with an aching gut. Take care of your health, they always said, and the rest takes care of itself. Which was almost true, he thought. Not quite, but very nearly. Stop the gut-ache if you can, and you'll sort out all your problems. Specially ones who like to gab a lot. Ones who think they've got away. Snotty little cunty ones.

He glanced at the clock on the wall. Gone one a.m., and the call hadn't come. But he didn't mind waiting, he was a patient man. He'd shaved and showered an hour ago. Chosen his grey silk suit, and his Chelsea boots. They made him taller, which always helped, for he liked to look his best, at times like these. Whatever happened, they should say of him: the fatman did it, and he was looking good.

A buzz came from the front of the house. He went into the hall and cocked an ear and his face creased into a smile. The night had barely started, and already they were bickering. He opened the door and waved them in, his boys, his lads, his protégés.

'Fucking cold out,' Billy muttered.

'You moaning, son?'

'I'm only saying.'

'Cause we know it's cold. Cause it's winter, see?'

'But I was only saying.'

'Well you've said it, right?'

They followed him into the drawing room. Billy parked himself in front of the fire, while Mervyn headed for the scotch.

'No booze,' Henry said.

'Just a small one, boss.'

He poured out three fingers of amber liquid.

'Just a weeny one,' he murmured.

The fatman's face remained impassive. You couldn't tell, by watching him, what he was feeling. You wouldn't know he had this burning deep inside. Like someone had struck a match and poked it in his belly, to see if it was flammable. You couldn't tell, by watching him. You might have guessed, if you were Mervyn, but you wouldn't know for sure.

'We having a party tonight, then?'

The fatman nodded.

'Something like that.'

'Just the three of us, is it?'

'Be a couple more later.' He lit a fag. 'Make up the numbers.'

'That's grand, boss, isn't it. Cause I like a good party.'

'I know you do. That's why we're having one.'

Mervyn took a swig of Johnnie Walker. He wiped his mouth.

'Be a few chicks, will there? Few nice girlies to pass around?'

'You partial, are you?'

'I'm Merv the Perv.'

The fatman nodded. Of course he was.

'There'll be everything, son. For me, I mean. You lads will just be watching.'

'Bit boring, watching.'

The fatman shrugged.

'Tough shit, old mate.'

And they spread themselves out, and settled down to wait. Henry smoking, Mervyn drinking, Billy picking his Billy spots. It was five to three when the call came through. Made them jump a bit, made them palpitate. Henry stubbed out his fag in an overflowing ashtray, and picked up the receiver on the seventh ring. He didn't interrupt. Kept his silence for half a minute, listened quietly for thirty seconds, being in a listening frame of mind. He glanced across. The boys were standing near the fire. They had that hopeful, eager, bloodhound look. They had a thuggish look, when you really looked.

He watched his lads, and spoke quietly into the phone. The murmured words of Henry when he's happy.

'That far out? . . . Yeah, sure. I know you have . . . No,' he muttered, 'we'll find it.'

He listened intently for several seconds.

'That's right. Just business.'

He scribbled some notes on a pad.

'Got it. You done great . . . I mean it, son . . . Yeah, I owe you.'

He replaced the phone. Didn't move for a while. Mervyn watched him carefully.

'That the party, boss?'

The fatman shuddered. It was a pleasure spasm, so he couldn't help it.

'It is, Merv.'

Almost giddy with delight, for this was the moment, the moment of moments.

'I knew we'd be having one,' he murmured softly. 'I just didn't know where.'

He crossed to the wall and unlocked the rosewood cabinet. It was where he kept his most precious things: the iron bars, the family photos, the locks of girly pubic hair. He reached inside and took out a velvet pouch, feeling the hard barrel beneath the soft material.

'Try and get sober, Merv. Always helps.'

The pistol slid out into his waiting hand.

'Cause we're going for a spin, see. A jolly little jaunt.'

He emptied the clip and checked the rounds.

'So better start the motor, Billy.'

He pushed the clip back in.

'There's a good lad.'

18

The rain came down spasmodically, at first. A softly deferential sound that spattered in her head and made her curl into a ball of foetal satisfaction. A mile or two away, across the scrubby grass and beyond the line of naked trees, a tractor engine almost fired. It sounded like an outboard motor, as if some farmer were yanking the cord, and every time it would almost fire, and every time it would suddenly die. Early morning in November, with the birdsong just beginning, and the half-light growing stronger, and the mist hanging low in a Hertfordshire field, and they're curled in the back of a wide-boy car, entwined in the back of a two-tone car.

She was half asleep and half awake, and the rain came drumming down. It hammered on the roof and bounced onto the ground. She felt Joe's breath against her neck, the heat of him beside her. The type of man who doesn't shave, who lets the darkness grow and gives his girl some trouble with his stubble. Better with him, his smell on her skin and his taste in her mouth, than kneeling before the fatman, bending the knee and bowing the head and kissing the fatman's cock.

For many things have happened to her, in her short and wholesome life. Many types have impinged themselves, have thrust themselves into her consciousness, have watched her raise her head above the grime and swiftly pushed it down again. They've shafted her as best they could, because they long to see her stumble, they ache to see her flounder, they yearn to see her fall. For though she is a sweet, young thing, a lot of people hate her, they loathe her absolutely. And she knows all this, the Donna bitch. She's a very knowing girl.

The rain came drumming down, a lazy flow that splashed onto the windscreen and forced its way beneath her skull, that trickled down the moulded glass and pushed inside her dream. She stretched, and yawned, and opened her eyes. Cold in the car. Joe slept on, his hand between her thighs. In the distance, the tractor engine almost turned. For a second it seemed that it almost fired. Her bones felt damp, the morning hunger gnawing at her belly.

A gentle tap on the window. She glanced outside. A bird, perhaps. Some country thing that flits above the grass. She heard the tap and glanced outside, saw shadows on the hood. Two trunk-like objects, planted on the hood. Rooted, as it were, a yard or so apart. Two muscled legs, standing on the hood.

And as she takes this in, as reality begins to seep into her brain, she notices the legs are wearing stonewashed denim jeans and high-neck leather boots, cherry-red and newly polished. She notices the rolling mist, the sullen light, the stream of yellow liquid drumming on the glass and dribbling neatly down. For Donna is the sort who notices these things.

And then there comes a revelation: the fundamental drawback of a two-door Ford Capri – a car with barely room enough for lovers to entwine themselves, to curl up in the rear and spend a night of almost bliss – the basic disadvantage is you're jammed inside the back, and there's nowhere you can run, and you're dreaming it's the rain while they're pissing on the glass, and suddenly you're conscious that the boys are here, they've come for you, the quietly vicious boys.

A mile or so across the fields, the engine turned, and failed, and almost died.

'Slags!'

The small black hole of Billy's mouth. It's early morning in November, with the birdsong just beginning, and the half-light growing stronger, and the mist hanging low in a Hertfordshire field, and you're curled in the back of a wide-boy car, entwined in the back of a two-tone car.

He hefted the crowbar above his head. The tractor motor suddenly fired. Vomit-panic churning in her belly. He braced himself. Pink-rimmed eyes in a bone-sharp face, and he's vibrant with hatred, he's throbbing with loathing.

'Pair of filthy fucking *slags*!'

A muted exhalation, a little scream of pleasure, and he swung the crowbar down. The windscreen exploded into the car. Golden drops and shards of glass seemed to hang in the air. Jagged noise erupted in her head. Something thudded against the side. She watched the driver's window caving in. Slow-motion, like the movies. They reached inside and flicked the lock, yanked open the door.

Joe glanced at her, the briefest second, his face a mask of perfect love and total fear. A fist smashed into the side of his head. She heard him shout her name. Again and again, like a mantra, as if her name could save him. An arm snaked in and grabbed him round the neck. They tipped the front seat down and heaved him over the top. She could hear him choking, someone laughing. A broad and unlined hand fluttered down onto his crotch. It paused a moment, as if in thought, then dug its hairless fingers in. And when she heard him scream, her life began to crumble, she watched her world disintegrate, the universe she'd built herself imploded.

'Come on, darling.'

The Billy murmur in her ear.

'Don't be shy.'

He reached inside and wrapped his fingers in her hair. He banged her head against the door and dragged her out, for he had permission from the fatman, authority to treat her rough. A special dispensation, on this very special day. There was a brief explosion of pale, grey sky, then mud in her face, and earth in her mouth, and the small, high grunts of skinhead glee as he hissed the cunt word, over and over.

19

Joe lay on the ground, softly groaning, the long grass flattened around him. Blood trickled out of his nose and mouth. His left eye was closed and beginning to go black. Mervyn was sitting on his chest. He bent forward, carefully cleared his throat, and allowed a thick gob of creamy phlegm to drop from his mouth.

'See that?' He sounded jubilant. 'Bang on the eyeball! Fucking brilliant!'

Henry leaned against the Daimler, his heavy shoulders drooping slightly, the plump legs crossed at the ankle. He was quietly watching, engorged with malice, putrescent with venom.

The November sky was hanging low above, a raw north wind came whipping against their skin, and everywhere the rich, damp smell, the dense and earthy odour, of a bare and unploughed field in Hertfordshire.

Billy grabbed her hair and pulled her up. Pus-faced Billy, having fun. He stared at her, just stared at her, his sandy lashes barely blinking. It made her tremble, the way he watched her. Made her flesh begin to quiver, and her bowels begin to melt, when he fixed her hard with his colourless eyes.

'I never liked you,' he remarked, 'to be quite honest.'

The words condensed in the frosty air, forming a cloud of vicious steam around his head.

'Never been a fan of yours, exactly.'

So close he was, they were nearly touching, almost kissing. She could see the flakes of dry skin that floated gently down from his forehead, the milky sediment that glistened in the corners of his eyes.

'I mean you think you're clever, don't you? Think you're such a genius.'

He clamped a hand around her neck.

'But I'll tell you something, sweetheart.'

The pitted flesh.

'I'm glad I'm not the Donna bitch. Not at this moment. Not right now.'

The razored scalp.

'Wouldn't want to be in your shoes, would I? Wouldn't want to be in your panties, see. Not there,' he said. 'Not me.'

A flash of perfect smile.

'Because it might be what one tends to call unpleasant.'

Saliva seeped between his lips, the bubbles forming and quietly bursting.

'Be fairly beastly, frankly. That's how I'd put it, if you asked me. If you really want to know.'

The grip of skinhead fingers round her neck.

'So what I'd like to convey,' he said, 'is how profoundly

glad I am that I'm not you. In fact,' he said, 'to put it more succinctly: at this precise and precious moment, in this field of frozen dung, I'm feeling rather grateful that I'm me.'

And having thus expressed himself, he shoved her face away.

'What's wrong with girly?'

Mervyn, fresh from working out with Joe, and sweating slightly, because he'd had to be firm, came sauntering over. He knew he was looking good, that day. Silk-lined coat and velvet collar. Scraped-clean nails and slicked-back hair. He knew he looked the business.

Billy frowned.

'What d'you mean, what's wrong?'

'I mean she's gone all grubby.'

'Has she?'

'Yeah.'

'Well some blokes like that type of thing.'

'Sort of mucky?'

Billy nodded.

'They like them dirty, frankly.'

'They'd like our girly, then.'

'They would.'

Mervyn leaned towards her. He held her chin and turned her face from side to side.

'But if I'm being honest, here . . .'

You could smell the toothpaste on his breath.

'. . . I'm not sure I'd want it myself, old mate.'

He peeled some grass from her lower lip.

'Not now we know where it's been.'

'It's been with Joe.'

'Precisely.'

'Gentlemen . . .'

The sudden rasp that cut the air.

'If one might interrupt, a moment . . .'

Billy shoved her forward.

'Gently does it.'

The fatman's voice, thick with satisfaction.

'Mustn't hurt her.'

He watched the skinhead tip his foot against her legs, and the Donna bitch was on her knees. A swollen Henry smile.

'You enjoying yourself, son?'

'I am, boss.'

''Cause we've barely started.'

'I know, boss.'

Henry gazed at her benignly.

'Look at me, darling.'

Billy took her by the hair and helped her raise her head. He pulled it back until she saw the broad and shining, pink and grinning, Henry face. The soft, wet mouth. The milky cheeks. The fatman in his glory.

'Been a while,' Henry murmured.

Rubbing his knuckles against his crotch.

'I mean it's been a while, since I've felt so good.'

The mist was thick above the field. He'll kill me now, she thought. She knew he wanted to, immensely. It was a private ache that filled the air, his need to do it, fairly soon.

He was smiling down.

'Speak to me, darling. Say something funny. Make a clever remark, you know the ones.'

He pointed to his left. Billy obligingly twisted her head. She saw Joe lying motionless on the ground.

'Didn't put up much of a fight, your bloke. Not very laddish, all things considering. Don't think I'm being critical, but he's what I'd call a tosser, frankly. Can't protect his girly, and I think she likes to be protected. Am I right, darling? Tell me, darling, am I right?'

He peered closer.

'What's that brown stuff you got in your mouth, eh? You got earth and grit in there, sweetheart. Grass and mud and shit like that. You got a lot of slime in there, precious, so better cough it out, why don't you.'

He shoved two fingers between her teeth.

'Just spit it out, the boys won't mind. That's my lovely. That's the way.'

He pushed his hand inside her mouth.

'Oh dear,' he said. 'Pity, that.'

He was gazing down, shaking his head.

'I always thought you were such a nice young girl. A cut above, if you take my drift. You sort of gave that impression, didn't you? Like you were something special, or something. And now you're puking on my shoes, without so much as a by-your-leave. I mean without even asking, and it's only polite to ask.'

'Piece of filthy—'

'Gag her, someone.'

The wind was cutting across the field. He shivered slightly. Pulled up his collar.

'Turning nippy, wouldn't you know it.'

He reached into the car and took out his thermos.

'Don't want to get a chill,' he murmured. 'Not at my age.'

He unscrewed the top and poured hot milk into the plastic cup.

'There's skin on that milk,' Mervyn said.

'I like it boiled, son. It's healthier.'

Mervyn shuddered.

'Can't abide milk skin. Makes me queasy.'

Henry shrugged.

'Each to his own.'

He sucked the liquid into his mouth, slowly swilled it round his gums.

'How you keeping, then, darling?'

His tongue darted out and licked the frothy rim from his lips.

'Been meaning to ask.'

He took another swig.

'Never quite got round to it, what with one thing and another.'

He drained the cup and screwed it back on.

'She's not saying much, is she?' Billy muttered.

'Not very talkative,' Mervyn added.

'And she does like to talk.'

'She does.'

'Maybe it's because she's got that thing in her mouth.'

'What thing?'

'That hankie thing. Got it stuffed inside her mouth . . .'

'Oh, yeah.'

'. . . and tied behind her head.'

'You think that's why she's keeping quiet?'

'I can't be sure, but it's possible.'

'Because she's always gabbing, never stopping.'

'Always with the mouth, the big, capacious mouth.'

'You've met her, then.'

'I have.'

'Boys . . .' Henry murmured. 'If I might have your attention, for a moment. If you'd care to gather round, I'd be obliged.'

Henry spread his arms indulgently, as though he would have embraced them all, as though he'd like to wrap them in his boundless love and squeeze them till they wept.

'We'd better start now, lads. Cause there's no point hanging round, not now we're ready.'

A quick glance round, just to be sure.

'We *are* all ready, I take it?'

Mervyn nodded.

'As ever, boss. Just say the word.'

'I'm saying it, Merv.'

He glanced at his watch.

'Let's stand them both together.'

They pulled Joe up and dragged him over, leaning him against the front of the Daimler. He was quietly moaning. Blood around his mouth. Henry smiled at the assembled group and slowly peeled off his gloves.

'So here we are again,' he murmured. 'Our merry little band.'

He stamped his feet and blew into his hands.

'Boys . . .' he began.

A courteous bow.

'Ladies . . .' he added gravely. 'Before we start, I should like to say a few words, cast some modest thoughts upon the water.'

He took out a packet of medium-strength.

'Because it seems to me it's rare enough that we're all together, chewing the cud and talking things over.'

He spread the tobacco on a small white square.

'The cut and thrust of honest debate.'

Rolled it between his fingers.

'So I just want to say, that whatever might occur, whatever might transpire . . .'

He licked the paper down.

'. . . I hope we'll still be friends.'

He tapped one end against his thumbnail, squeezed the other, and placed the roll-up between his lips.

'And I'd like you all to know', he said, 'that I don't blame Joey. Cause he was a good little lad, till she came along. A polite little bleeder, till she came along.'

He gazed at her.

'You listening, darling? Cause I'm talking, darling.'

He struck a match, holding the flame to the end of the fag.

'Pull her up, Billy. Think she's sagging again. Lift up her head, so she can get a good look.'

The bright red tip as he sucked in heat.

'Some people, see, you try to help them, you do your level best to extend to them a helping hand.'

The muted crackle of burning tobacco.

'And what do they do? They trash your car, they steal your dough, they stick their fanny in your face and gaily walk away. What I'd term ungrateful people. Think they're not accountable. Don't realize they're beholden.'

He flicked off ash.

'They never seem to understand that they're alive, they're breathing on this earth, because I've got a tender heart. I've got what's called a tender, beating heart, and I let them live a while. I let them go about their business. I let them fuck, and fart, and think they've got a purpose.'

He shook his head.

'And because I didn't tread on them, because I didn't stamp my foot and smear them on the pavement, they think they'll get away with it, they think that they're immortal, they think they'll screw the fatman.'

Billy's fingers in her hair, the head jerked back, arms flapping by her side. The big man moved forward, stopping a foot or so in front of her.

'It's very sad', he said gently, 'that you've brought us down to this. I mean I like to think we're civilized, and look what you're making us do.'

His cheeks caved in as he took a drag.

'You've been a bad girl,' he said, 'so I'm going to teach you a lesson.'

He blew a thoughtful smoke ring in the air.

'I'm going to teach you to be good.'

He dropped the cigarette on the ground.

'One will be punished, and one will watch.'

We are nothing, she realized. Weightless, on this earth.

'One will fall, and one will be saved.'

Oh mother, come and help me now.

His piggy eyes flicked between them, as if making a rapid calculation, as if he knew what would happen and was merely playing out some ritual, some bizarre game that only he understood, and that only he could win.

He pointed a finger at Donna.

'Eeny.'

Swung it towards Joe.

'Meeny.'

Back at her.

'Miney.'

Slowly swivelled back to Joe.

'Mo.'

A contented fatman sigh.

'I'm afraid you've drawn the short straw,' he said. 'Bad luck, old son.'

He unbuttoned his coat.

'The belly, Mervyn, if you wouldn't mind.'

Joe's arms were pinned behind him, and Henry slipped a piece of moulded steel around his knuckles. Taking his time, for he was a careful man, he drew back his arm, glanced at the girl, and then the sudden thud of metalled fist on unprotected flesh. Mervyn released an ecstatic gasp. Joey's legs began to buckle. Billy held her very tight.

'You know why I do these things, don't you.'

He removed the knuckleduster and slipped it back in his pocket.

'Because I can,' he explained. 'And as I can, I will.'

They flipped Joe round and pushed him down over the bonnet. Banged his head hard on the frost-covered metal. Mervyn leaned his weight across Joe's shoulders.

'Bring her nearer,' Henry ordered.

He was gazing down admiringly at his white and hairless hands.

'Should've been a pianist,' he muttered. 'Don't you reckon, Merv? Would've been quite good at that, giving concerts and stuff. Easy money, once they know you.'

Mervyn nodded.

'Just learn a few tunes and you're laughing, right?'

Henry stared at him.

'You trying to be funny?'

'Boss?'

''Cause they're cultured people, fuckhead. And we're partial to culture, aren't we, son.'

'Yeah, boss. Sure.'

A soft and rueful fatman sigh. That a man like him should have to consort with types like that. It pained him, sometimes. Made his insides contract.

'They give *pleasure*, Merv, and one finds one's pleasures where one can.'

Which train of thought returned him to the task in hand, and he fixed his gaze on his former driver. The sudden wave of fatman pity. I'm good, he thought. I'm a decent bloke.

'You thought it was the worst thing, didn't you?'

Speaking softly, almost gently.

'The most hideous thing that could ever happen, when they tied that string around your knob and pulled you round at play-time.'

He shook his head. He empathized.
'But there are worse things on this earth, Joe.'
Slowly undoing his tie.
'There's always something worse, in life.'

20 _____

She'd thought it would be her, at first. Thought they'd pass her round and share her out, they'd dip their noses in her goodies and have a furtive poke around. But when she saw the hands around Joe's waist, the belt unbuckled, jeans dragged down below his knees, something oozed, unbidden, into her brain, a shameful, dirty, Donna thought. They're doing it to him, she thought. Thank God, she thought, it won't be me.

The big man watched her as he opened his flies.

'Remember this?'

His cock in his hand.

'You know how I'm feeling now, darling? Mellow, is how I'm feeling. I'm finally at peace with myself, my love.'

He passed his tongue between his lips.

'No-one needs to know,' he confided. 'It'll be our little secret.'

With which remark he bent and covered his former driver, his red hair flopping forward, making sure that she was watching him as he shoved himself inside. He gazed at her and smiled at her, even might have winked at her.

'What they value most,' he breathed, 'is what I tend to take.'

And then he was lost in the perfect moment. Sweat broke out on his jowly face, his mouth sagged open, and he was grunting as he thrusted, jerking back and forth with the manic concentration of a dog that's rutting in the park.

When you scream through a gag, the noise that you make won't bring anyone running. Even if you weren't abandoned in a field, there's no-one who'll come running if you're screaming through a gag. It's a strangulated sound, a kind of smothered, high-pitched whine that echoes in your mouth and slips back down your throat.

Makes them laugh, though, when you do it. They like it when they hear you howl. They like to hear the Donna bitch debase herself.

'She trying to distract us?'

'I think she is.'

'She's always been selfish.'

'Always has to spoil it.'

'Not a nice girl, is she.'

'Not very, no.'

A couple more minutes and then he finished, for even Henry had his limits, even the fatman could have enough. He heaved himself off and buttoned himself up, and the boys were still standing, staring, wanting more.

'That'll teach him.'

'Stupid shit deserved it.'

'Fucking poofter.'

'Lucky cunt, then, wasn't he.'

Henry wiped his forehead with his coatsleeve.

'Language, boys,' he chided. 'Ladies present.'

He eased his gloves carefully on, for they were quality leather, and they fitted well. He looked contented, gently sated. He looked like he looked when he'd just had a feed. When he'd just stuffed his face, and was full of goodwill. He glanced at the girl. Fixed her with his piggy eye.

'I'm not a bad person,' he remarked.

He draped his cashmere scarf around his neck.

'Just a bit impulsive.'

The lank and sweat-soaked hair.

'But I mean well, don't I. And that's what counts.'

Mist was slowly rolling in. The frost on the grass was melting.

'Better be off then,' he murmured. 'Got to get back to the smoke.'

He watched the boys climb into the Daimler.

'Various matters to attend to. Things to sort out. You know what I mean.'

His breath formed insubstantial clouds around his head.

'Time to say ta-ra then, sweetheart. Got to love you and leave you.'

He bent slightly. Red hair in her face.

'Keep in touch, why don't you.'

He kissed her gently on the cheek.

'That's what friends are for.'

21

She watched the car recede into the distance, listened to the sound of its engine as it became lower, and softer, and gradually disappeared. The field was thick with sudden silence, a shrill and vacant emptiness that forced its way inside her head, as though they'd driven a nail into the skull, hammered it into the bone. No-one left but her and Joe. Dust and garbage. Weightless, on this earth.

The mist was beginning to thicken. Soon it would be difficult to make out his features. You wouldn't be able to read him any more. You'd only be able to see the shape, standing by the car.

'Getting cold,' she murmured.

His jacket was lying, neatly folded, by his feet. She didn't know if she should pick it up. She wanted him to tell her what to do, because things like that she doesn't know. Things like what you're meant to do when the boys have been and gone, and the jacket's lying by his feet, and he's standing quietly by the car.

So Joe, she thought, so tell me, Joe . . .

'Turning frosty,' she said.

The nail inside her skull.

'Be turning nasty, fairly soon.'

The wind was slicing across the field. He was standing in his shirtsleeves, staring at the ground. She watched his face and tried to guess what he was feeling, what might, at that precise and putrid second, be spilling through his brain.

'Better be starting back,' she said, 'start heading back to town.'

She hunched her shoulders and blew on her hands. Just keep on talking, fill the silence.

'I'll drive, if you want. Always been a decent driver. But we've got to get back, Joe, got to get started. I mean it's getting foggy, so we better get back to town. Lie low for a bit, go find a doctor. Have to go now, Joe, cause I can't abide the country, see. It's not me,' she said, 'not quite my thing.'

The nail embedded in her skull.

'All the green, I reckon. Bit too countrified. Can't bear it, really, don't know why. So what d'you say then, Joey? What d'you reckon, Joe?'

She could hear her voice. Such a stupid voice.

'We making a move?'

He began to button his shirt. The slightest tightening of his lips.

'I don't need a doctor.'

His voice was quiet, without inflection. When he bent to pick up the jacket, she heard him gasp, the sort of stifled sound one makes when a wound is stretched. You wouldn't have heard it, unless you were listening. A brief, astonished intake of breath, when he bent and picked up the jacket.

'I think you'd better go now.'

He took out his cigarettes.

'I think you'd better,' he said.

The nail inside her skull.

'Just leave me now.'

'All right.'

She didn't move.

'Joe . . . ?' she whispered. 'What'll you do, now, Joe?'

Because she has to know. Because she has no tact, she has no sense of waiting for the moment. For Donna has this clarity of vision, she has this pure and true perception. She knows that if they damage you, you have to take revenge. She knows that when they split you open, when they push inside and poke around, you have to feel complete again, clear out all the dirt.

That's what she knows, the Donna bitch. Avenge yourself or die. Make them weep, or slit your wrist, just take a knife and lie down in a steaming bath and slit your tiny wrist. For better dead, is how she'd put it. Better in the earth and feeding worms, better just a memory, than like a dog they lead around. Better do it, frankly. Better finish it, just end it, fairly quickly, if you'd rather let them live.

'Joe . . .'

For nothing much had changed. It was merely made concrete what had once been abstract, confirmed with flesh and blood what had always been known but left unsaid: that Joe was born for violation, someone destined to be shafted. It was written, as they say. It was printed on his forehead at the moment of conception: this man is put on earth to swallow what you give him. We let him live because he'll lick his plate and smile, because he'll bend the knee and bow the head and eat the muck we set before him. So every day of Joey's life he's fed a little piece of excrement. A tiny piece, to educate his palate.

'Joe . . .' she said, 'I'm sorry, Joe.'

And they trained him well. They must have told him when he was a boy, a little lad so full of sweetness. They must have whispered in his ear: You're nothing, Joe. You're less than zero. Made him used to it. Accustomed him to hearing he was something lesser, someone to be pissed on, a piece of dreck they stepped in by mistake. Joey growing up and never fitting in. Squeeze his balls and make him cry. Tie some string around his cock and lead him round the playground. But all in fun, they only jest, a bit of laddish humour. Because they've fucked him all his life, been shafting him since he was small. Spread him out and shoved inside, so it's nothing new, not too surprising. Joey playing host again. Welcoming his friends.

'My fault . . .' she said.

He shrugged.

'Rather me than you, though.'

Bitter smile on Joey's face. All broken mouth and bitter smile.

'That what you're thinking, is it? Better it was Joey-boy, cause that's what Joey's for?'

You could hardly bear to look at him. He had a crumpled, flattened look, a kind of rubbish look, a look of pure, unblemished impotence. The look of someone who'd been bent and spread, who'd been well and truly entered by his betters.

The wind came scything across the field and forced its way inside her mouth.

'Joe . . .'

She touched his shoulder. The barest touch, which barely made him quiver.

'You should get in the car,' he muttered. 'Catch cold out here.'

'I don't mind.'

'Don't want you getting a chill,' he said.

She shook her head, trembled in the wind.

'We driving into town, then, Joe? We going now? We off now, Joey?'

He didn't even look at her. Kept staring at the ground.

'I don't think so really.' He shook his head. 'I don't think we should do things like that.'

'Like driving . . .'

'Do things together. I don't think so, no.'

The nail inside her skull.

'I think we should do things apart,' he said. 'Makes sense, really. Better split, I mean. We're different, now.'

'Still the same.'

'Can't say I agree with you, there. Not really of one mind, I'm afraid. So we'd better say adieu.'

The rusted nail inside her skull.

'So I'll see you then,' he said. 'Been fun, I guess.'

'You mean I—'

'I mean you'd better go,' he said.

He placed a fag between his lips.

'I think you'll find that's what I mean.'

22

The air was bad in there as she tried to recall the number, the receiver cold against her ear. She looked outside, saw thick, grey cloud hanging low above the rooftops. It was fat and bloated, pressing down. So close it was, she could have stabbed it. Could have ripped it open, if she'd had a blade.

Donna in stiletto heels, standing in the booth. You couldn't tell by watching her, couldn't guess by looking at her face the kind of thought the Donna bitch was thinking. You'd have to get inside her, have to crack the fragile skull and touch the pulpiness inside, hammer on the shell to reach the brainy bits inside. So you couldn't tell, if you'd have seen her, that she had this vacant feeling in her belly, a void and puked-out feeling, a sense of being finished, gutted, empty. Her and Joey. Dust and garbage. Nothing, on this earth.

She punched out the number and waited. There was a

Y-shaped crack in the middle window, as if someone had banged his head against the glass, as if he'd simply had enough, and had rammed his bovine head against the British Telecom glass.

The phone rang three times, was answered on the fourth. That smooth, familiar voice. She shut her eyes. Nothing, on this earth. Less than nothing. Minus nothing. Weightless, on this earth.

'Hello, Henry.'

Speaking quietly. Nice and docile.

'It's me.'

A soft release of breath, a sigh of almost pleasure, came floating down the line. She could almost hear the cogs begin to whirr inside his brain. She could almost hear him spread his legs, and touch his groin, and quietly tell himself: the bitch is back.

'Nice to hear from you, sweetheart.'

Easing himself back in the padded chair.

'Been wondering when you'd get in touch.'

The smirk came seeping down the line.

'So how's my little luscious?'

The tongue felt swollen in her mouth.

'I'm . . . I want to come back.'

Something pale and viscous glistened on the floor. A small and perfect pool of sputum. A souvenir gobbed up the day before.

'Course you do,' he murmured. 'Not got many options, darling. Just a sweet young thing who's good in bed. Who's always known, from an early age, that her fanny would be her fortune.'

The vacant feeling in her belly. The sense of being finished, gutted, empty.

'So sell it while you can, my love. Milk it, while we want it. That's what girlies do, when they've got no other choice. They take what's being offered. They bend the knee, and bow the head, and walk the trodden path.'

She could smell herself, the mud on her clothes and the sick on her blouse. She could smell the stink of Donna bitch.

'Please . . .'

Nothing, on this earth.

'Have to think a bit,' he said. 'Have to sit and cogitate.'

The damp was leaking into her bones. Making them soft. Making them porous. He could have pressed his thumb against her spine and pushed it gently in, he could have made an indentation in her vertebrae.

'You'll have to forget the lad,' he said.

'Already forgotten.'

Bend the knee and bow the head.

'Don't want him, any more.'

'Didn't think you would. Thought you might have cooled, a bit.'

'Things are different, now.'

'I know they are. I spoiled your goods. I went inside and spoiled your goods.'

Cold inside the booth. A whiff of urine in the air.

'So what's the problem, darling?'

'Got no money,' she whispered. 'Feeling bad.'

'Tell me something new,' he said. 'You've been running round with rubbish, see? Eating slop and sleeping rough. Living like a pig.'

The ooze of fatman happiness.

'I know,' she said. 'He led me on.'

'So I did him for you.'

'Brought me to my senses.'

'Big soft lad, and I sorted him out.'

'You did him, Henry. Did him hard.'

'And I'll tell you something.'

'Tell me, Henry.'

'Shall I tell you, darling?'

'Tell me, Henry.'

'He liked it, didn't he.'

That urine smell. That all-pervading urine smell.

'Fucking loved it, if you're asking.'

The gob on the floor and the smell in the air.

'Ought to kiss my calfskin boots. Just go down on his knees and kiss my fucking boots, cause I did the boy a favour.'

She could hear him smiling down the phone. And once again that thought, that dirty Donna thought: he who doesn't crave to bury his tormentors is maybe better in the earth, where he can slowly putrefy. For if he doesn't ache for retribution, not even in the privacy of damp and clammy dreams, not even then, not even fantasize, not even privately, he's maybe better dead. They'd better finish him completely. Just snuff him out and melt him down and spread him on the vegetables. Just put him in a petticoat and lay him in the ground. Just shove it in and walk away. Just fuck him and forget him.

'Want to come back . . .' she muttered.

'I'll think about it.'

'Back where I belong . . .'

'Have to have a little think.'

'Please . . .' she urged.

'I mean you've given me a lot of grief, the last few days. Made me lose my temper. Made me get my tool out in a frozen field in Hertfordshire.'

'I'm sorry, Henry.'

'You'll have to prove it.'

That vacant feeling in her belly. The sense of being finished, gutted, empty.

'Got to make amends,' he said, 'because you let him in, my

love. Turned me down, and let him in. Now I'm not the type who holds a grudge, I'm not what's termed vindictive, but that upset me, frankly. Made me kick some doors in, and I'm not too fond of hooligans. So I had to make things right again. Had to teach you both a lesson. I mean I like to think of us as friends, but sometimes even friends require a spanking. Stands to reason, really. Firm but fair, is what I am. So there we are,' he said, 'and off we go.'

'And you'll take me back . . .'

'Long as you behave,' he said. 'I like my girlies when they're good.'

'Can I . . . may I say something?'

'Of course you may.'

'You didn't have to do it, Henry.'

'But that's the point, my love. It was what we call gratuitous.'

She's swaying on her feet. Taste of metal in her mouth.

'So I'm coming round . . . ?'

'Merv'll bring you. You can meet him somewhere handy. Nice boy, Merv. Quite fond of you. He'll bring you round.'

'Can't I come straight over?'

'Better not.'

Grinning down the line.

'Just in case,' he said. 'We don't want any . . . incidents. Might get impulsive, darling. Might do something silly. Lose your head and get carried away, you know the way you do.'

'I'm different now.'

'I know you are. But you come round here, and you've got to behave.'

She heard a faintly oily sound, as thick and placid lips were brought together. The sound of Henry being happy. Anticipation at the thought of lubrication.

'We'll do it tomorrow. Give you time to have a bath.

Tomorrow, you go up Leicester Square. The Gaumont, right? Get a ticket for Screen Three. You got enough for a ticket?'

'Yes.'

'The early evening programme,' he said.

'Lunchtime,' she murmured.

'What?'

'Don't like the dark.'

'Two o'clock, then. Shouldn't be too crowded. Just sit upstairs, right at the back, and he'll come and find you. Whatever he says, you do it, right? And don't cause trouble, cause you know what he's like when you're difficult.'

The rustle of cellophane.

'You'll have a chat, then he'll bring you round.'

'And we'll start again?'

'We will.'

The sound of a cigar stuffed in his mouth.

'How was Joey, when you left him?'

'All right,' she said. 'A bit depressed.'

The Henry chuckle.

'Don't blame him, frankly, cause if I were him – and thank fuck I'm not – a bit depressed is what I'd be. And I'll tell you something for nothing, shall I? If he were half a man, he'd kill himself. He had any balls, he'd top himself. Cause it's disgusting, what he did. Makes me sick to my fucking stomach. You know what I'm saying? Cause I've been *in* there, darling. Gone tunnelling inside.'

The click of the lighter.

'Your boy's been had, my love.'

The hiss of smoke sucked down the lungs.

'He's been shafted, well and truly.'

23

She didn't sleep much, that night. Sleep didn't creep up and steal her away. She'd found a bedsit behind King's Cross, and lay there wide-eyed in the dark. She stared at the ceiling and chewed her lip, for there was nothing to do but wait till daylight. Undressed, derobed, ensconced between the sheets, sleep eluded her through a long, black night. Just engines revving on the street, and music leaking through the wall, and every time she shut her eyes the endless field in Hertfordshire.

Maybe she snatched an hour or two, she couldn't tell. All she knew, it was gone eleven, the room was cold, and her brain felt thick with unfinished dreams. She pushed back the blanket and stared at the ceiling. Thin brown cracks had fissured the plaster. A lorry was reversing down below, and diesel fumes came seeping through the window.

She rolled out of bed and took a lukewarm shower, then

pulled on a skirt and a tight, black top. Her Henry outfit, as it were. Clothes to please a fatman. Lunch was taken across the road. Just buttered toast and a cup of tea, for she wasn't in an eating mood, not of a mind to gorge herself. She took her time though, didn't rush. Read the paper, and checked the horses, and all the while the vague, obscure awareness that someone might be watching.

It didn't take long to get into town. Thirty minutes, more or less. She took a bus to Euston, then tubed it down to Leicester Square. Gaudy, filthy Leicester Square. The crowds were bad that day, a fluid mass of scabby tourists eating burgers. Walking slowly, taking up space. You could hardly move for rucksacks, and she had that hemmed-in feeling you get in London, that surge of claustrophobic rage that bubbles up inside until you think you might erupt, until you throb and ache for self-expression. She could have let them know, could have taken one aside and explained it, very carefully, but there were other things to think about, other factors to consider. She had a rendezvous with Mervyn, so she had to save her energy.

By the time she reached the Gaumont, the theatre was dark, the picture just beginning. Barely twenty seats were taken, for which she thanked her deity. She wrinkled her nose and sniffed the air. It didn't smell too bad, for once. Not too reeking, as it happened. It didn't have that whiff of strangers packed together, that stink you get when they've rushed off on a Friday night to watch the latest from the States, when they're crammed in tight and sit there sweating in the gloom.

She took a seat three rows from the back, near the left-hand aisle. You wouldn't have seen her, unless you were looking, for she was trying not to push herself. Demure, you'd call her, if you passed her. Fairly self-effacing. The nearest person was eight rows down, which was how she liked it. No point getting close, unless one really had to. No point interacting, prematurely.

She placed her handbag on the floor. Tried to focus on the story. He'd get there soon, with his slicked-back hair and his Fulham smile. Maybe gloating. Maybe not. She stared at the image on the screen. Her guts felt raw. Have to eat, she thought, got to take in fuel. Iron band around her chest, and the blood was pounding in her head.

She shut her eyes, saw Joey lying on the ground, scarlet trickling from his mouth. Mervyn squatting, toad-like, on his stomach. He clears his throat, then the gob of creamy phlegm and *bang on the eyeball, fucking brilliant.* The field, the mist, the grinning boys. *Can't abide milk skin. Makes me queasy.* He leans towards her, sniffs the air. *Cause if I'm being honest, here . . .* She could smell the toothpaste on his breath . . . *I'm not sure I'd want it myself, old mate.*

She opened her eyes. The fatman smiling. *The belly, Mervyn, if you wouldn't mind.* She stared at the screen. The endless field, the grinning boys. Iron band around her chest, and the blood kept pounding in her head, and—

'Hello, darling.'

All shower gel and aftershave. He checked the rows in front and behind, then eased himself down beside her.

'Keeping well?'

'Getting by.'

'That's nice,' he said.

He picked up her bag and zipped it open.

'I'm glad you're getting by,' he said.

He shoved a hand inside and rummaged round.

'Because if you weren't quite getting by, I might be worried.'

He zipped the bag shut, let it drop to the floor.

She felt him staring in the dark.

'So here we are,' he said, 'the two of us.'

Legs spread wide. So cool, he was. Such a total lad. A smart, young thug with attitude. He took out a hip flask and unscrewed the cap.

'You back on the brandy?'

'Passes the time.'

He told her how he'd dressed up just for her, got smartened up especially. Put on his best grey suit and his Chelsea boots, stuck a fobwatch in the waistcoat pocket. For her, he stressed. He'd done it all for girly.

She listened as he swigged it back, heard it sloshing down the tube.

'You enjoying that, are you?'

He wiped his mouth with the back of his hand.

'Always had a noisy swallow.'

'Is that a fact?'

'Been told I got it from my mum.'

'Didn't know you had a mum, Merv.'

'You don't know much, then.'

'Thought you might have been found on someone's doorstep. Thought you sort of *appeared* one day. Like a herpe.'

He shook his head.

'No, sugar. Just dropped out the hole and there I was.'

'Must've been nice for her.'

'I think it was.'

'I mean, nine whole months . . .'

'. . . and then there's me.'

They sat there quietly for a moment, contemplating motherhood, and then she said:

'Business all right, is it?'

'It's booming, sweetheart. Money's fucking rolling in. Got too much, sometimes. Don't know what to do with it. Got it coming out my ears, and things. I mean I go round on the pickup and I have to take a briefcase, don't I. And I hate doing that, cause it makes me look like I'm flogging insurance, like I'm some wanky salesman, some yuppie tit from Docklands.'

He frowned.

'Which I'm not.'

She watched the movement on the screen.

'You got it with you?'

'The briefcase . . . ?'

'The money.'

'No.'

'Oh.'

He slipped the hip flask back in his pocket.

'So I'll be walking back to the car, see, carrying a good few grand, and I'm thinking, am I going to be mugged today? Is today my mugging day?'

'You waste your brain on stuff like that?'

'Course I do.'

'But you're a *yob*,' she hissed.

He looked at her reproachfully.

'Yobs have feelings too, you know.'

'Well you needn't worry.'

'You reckon, do you?'

'I mean you won't be mugged. It's not going to happen.'

'Not ever?'

'Never.'

'You sure of that?'

'I'm positive. I've got this feeling in my fanny.'

He smiled at her.

'You been thinking of me?'

'Each waking moment.'

'I'm warming to you, darling. I'm liquefying, at this moment.'

'Well don't start dripping.'

He touched her cheek.

'Such a sweet young face, and such a dirty mouth.'

'Have I?'

'What?'

'A sweet young face?'

He didn't answer, just inched towards her.

'You know what I've got to do now, my love?'

He began clicking his knuckles, perhaps out of habit.

'Got to search you, sugar, so just relax.'

He was leaning over, blocking the picture.

'Pat you down, then off we go.'

So slim she was, he could wrap a hand round both her wrists.

'Pockets first, if you wouldn't mind.'

You could almost hear his wide-boy grin.

'Then all your little nooks and crannies.'

She kept her eyes on the screen while he felt her. Kept them locked on the screen while his palms pressed over, and under, and slowly around. He frisked her very carefully, taking his time, a methodical man. Like kids they were, like a courting couple, clamped together in the dark.

'Sorry, sweetheart, but I'm only checking. Have to be sure, see . . .'

The brandy gusting from his mouth.

'. . . have to be certain.'

He slipped a hand beneath her skirt. A rueful shrug.

'Henry's orders, what can I tell you.'

His fingers brushed against her crotch.

'Enjoy yourself, he said. You have a good time, he said. Just keep it tasteful, cause we don't want any scenes, old son, we don't want the punters getting distressed. That's what we truly do not want.'

He pressed his mouth against her neck and murmured in her ear.

'I mean we both know Henry, don't we? Likes to observe the

niceties, see. Got his sense of fatman decorum. So I'll do my best, I said. Anything for a mate, I said. So here we are, and away we go.'

He felt her moisten through the cotton and allowed himself a grunt of satisfaction.

'Just remember, right? I'm not like Billy. Because I've always liked you, haven't I? Basically, I mean. You know that, don't you?'

'That you like me?'

'Deep down,' he said.

'Down where?'

'Down there.'

The fingers wormed between her thighs.

'Be mine,' he breathed.

'My heart belongs to Henry.'

'But your cunt belongs to me.'

'I want the colonel, not the corporal.'

'Not a nice remark.'

She removed his hand and placed it in his lap.

'Never said I was nice, Merv.'

He leaned his head towards her. Whispered in her ear.

'You want to forget him, precious. He's an old man, see, and they shouldn't let the old do things like that. It's what I'd class as out of order. Makes me shudder, frankly. Should be a law against it, if you want my opinion.' He quietly sniffed. 'And even if you don't.'

'You think you'd make me happy, Merv?'

'I think you'd be ecstatic.'

'And you'd do what I want . . . ?'

'I'd do anything you asked.'

A cautious glance.

'Within reason, that is.'

She nodded slowly. Sounded fair enough. She fixed her gaze on the screen, and said:

186

'So you'd kiss it, would you?'

A sudden intake of wide-boy breath as he mulled this over in his brain, and then he murmured:

'Course I would.'

He smoothed down his tie and examined his nails.

'You pay me enough, and I'll kiss it for you.'

She shook her head.

'I never pay for it, darling.'

He shrugged his shoulders.

'And I never kiss it, sweetheart.'

They grinned at each other in the cosseting dark, almost friendly, almost bonding.

'Glad you're coming back,' he said. 'Thought maybe you wouldn't, after what happened . . .'

She looked confused.

'Sorry, Merv? Miss something, did I?'

'The other day,' he prompted. 'That bit of unpleasant-ness . . .'

'Oh, that.' She pulled a face. 'One of those things.'

'Yeah,' he said. 'What I thought, too.'

He glanced at the screen. It was a kiddies' movie, and he'd seen it before.

'Hope Joey didn't mind too much, cause it was just a laugh, see, a bit of fun. So I hope he's not gone off in a sulk, hope he's not going to be an arsehole . . .'

Pause for unembarrassed burp.

'. . . no pun intended.'

Hot in there. He loosened his collar.

'How is he, anyway? Bit green round the gills? Bit pink round the edges? Bit tender, is he? A bit inflamed? Because he should have used some Nivea, shouldn't he. You tell him from me, so he'll know for next time – he should smear on the cold cream and it won't be so bad. Just ponce along to Boots and buy himself a large-size tub. Tell him Mervyn said, and give him my best. We were mates, see, darling. That's why I care.'

He slid himself down, made himself comfortable.

'So tell me, darling, how's your lad?'

A soft voice floated from behind:

'Surviving.'

A nylon wire flicked through the air. Mervyn lifted slightly in his seat. His body gently arched, the legs began to tremble, and Joe was leaning forward, head bent low so he's nearly butting, almost kissing, grinning hard through gritted teeth, quietly weeping as he pulled the cords, as he crossed his hands and pulled them tight.

The ripples spread along the seats and made them shake, as in a train. It felt like sitting in the train when it goes over the points, when two tracks merge and the wheels almost jump. The train begins to shudder as it cuts across the intersection, and you feel it in your seat, you feel the movement in your seat. It spreads across your back and between your legs, and everyone's staring at the floor because the train's vibrating in their crotch, which makes them happy, for a moment. Or at least contented, if they're hard to please.

It didn't take long, once Joey started. Ninety seconds, give or take. You'd think it might take longer, but it didn't. Even someone like Mervyn, someone in a pale grey three-piece suit, with a fobwatch in his waistcoat pocket, in handmade shoes and aftershave, with a tasty business up and running, a well-dressed yob with slicked-back hair, even such a man can still be snuffed out fairly quickly.

You have to get up right behind him, though. You've got to come up close behind, and you slip the cord around his neck and quickly pull it tight. But nice and smoothly, nothing nasty. Then you listen to the sound he makes. You tilt your head, and cock an ear, and listen very carefully. The final, mortal gurgle of the one who held you down. And you realize something, if you're Joey. Your brain kicks into gear again, and you realize something beautiful. They've always said revenge is sweet. But it's more than sweet. It's a crème brûlée.

He didn't look like a dead man when they'd finished. People see what they expect to see, and you don't expect to see a dead man in the Gaumont, Leicester Square. Comatose, perhaps, but not quite dead. She'd brought along the evening paper, and she covered his face, for decency. Then she slid a hand inside his jacket, fumbling for the holster. He hadn't brought along his dosh, but he'd remembered to bring his automatic. Bastard hadn't brought the money, but at least he'd brought his pistol, bless him.

She gave herself three blissful seconds to hold it in her hand – a loaded, matt-black pistol in her small and dainty hand – then dropped it in her bag and zipped it neatly shut.

'We going, Joe?'

He didn't answer. He took her by the arm and they walked up the aisle and into the foyer. Keep on moving, they'd agreed. Look self-absorbed, and don't look back. So they're quietly talking, almost smiling, just two young sweethearts on a date.

Into the street, and the comforting roar of a confident city, the reassuring stink of Leicester Square. She watched the girls go walking by. Not like me, she thought, they're none of them like me, she thought. They haven't sat there in the dark, with Mervyn's thigh pressed hard against their own, with Mervyn's smell, and Mervyn's scent and Mervyn right beside them, and felt their lover strangle him, felt him be garrotted, felt the man they let inside pull tight on both the cords. Choke the air from Mervyn's lungs. Snuff him out entirely.

Joe led her down a side road, took a left, then left again, and they were in a yard, an unlocked space with cardboard boxes and polystyrene.

'Where's this?' she said.

'Just somewhere quiet.'

He had a bloodless face. Cadaverous, almost. Worse than Mervyn, if one's honest. She touched his hand.

'You all right?'

'Yeah, I'm all right.'

Pale blue sky and winter sun. Just him and her and an empty courtyard.

'So what now, then, Joey?'

'Thought we'd play a game.'

'You mean another one?'

'Yeah, another one.'

'What kind of game?'

'It's called the can-be game. Know it, do you?'

She shook her head.

'It's simple, really, got very few rules. I mean it's all a matter of who I can be. Cause I can be Joe, or I can be Henry.'

She gazed at him, at the broken mouth and the drained-out eyes.

'Be Joey, Joey.'

His body seemed slowly to shrivel. He became smaller, rounder, feminized. A sweet young boy, not one to take advantage.

'May I kiss you?'

He held her hand so gently she could barely feel it, barely feel the pressure of his fingers on her skin. Didn't press or rub against her, didn't want to take what wasn't freely given.

'May I hold you?'

The one she loved, the self-effacing one she loved.

'Be Henry, Joey.'

He wrapped his fingers in her hair, jerked back her head and jammed his broken mouth on hers. He pushed his tongue between her teeth and rubbed his groin, his hard, hot groin, against her crotch. Then he pressed her back against the wall, pulled down her tights and pushed himself inside, he shoved himself inside, he pressed his mouth against her neck and tunnelled his way inside.

24

Billy eyed the daughter uneasily. Every time she passed she seemed to brush against him. Nothing obvious, not so close he could shove her off. Not her, he thought, too fucking smart. She'd just sidle past and brush him with her fingers, sometimes with her hips, her large and generous hips, which made it even worse. So Rubenesque she was it made him want to gag, just stick his fingers down his throat and gently retch. For he didn't like them round like that. The curves got on his nerves.

He'd parked his car down the Lambeth Road, and was saying hello to Albert, passing the time of day in Albert's cash-and-carry. Bonding, so to speak. He always went there, of a Friday. Nice and regular, never fail. Every week, come rain or shine, like a healthy bowel movement. Bit of certainty in an uncertain world. You wanted Billy on a Friday, you had to shoot across the water, you had to trickle down to Lambeth, for there the lad would be.

So he's in the office behind the shop, nursing a mug of milky tea and eyeing the plate of assorted biscuits. A small heap of banknotes lay on the desk, a little pile of tens and twenties waiting for collection. Old man Albert was sitting opposite, holding his cup while his daughter poured.

'Enough!' he hissed. 'I said *enough!*'

She banged the teapot down. Lulu, her name was, the skinhead reflected. A touch assertive, unlike her dad. Lulu by name, and lulu by nature. Chestnut hair, which she combed a lot. Fourteen years old and a total pubescent. Hormones, he shuddered. Excessive secretions. When he stole a glance to check if she'd grown, he found her gazing back at him. Got a cheek, he thought. Got a fucking nerve.

'All right, then, Lulu?'

'Fine, thanks, Billy.'

The tea was burning him through the mug.

'School nice, is it?'

'OK,' she said. 'Did Social Trends, today. About gangs and stuff, and why people join.'

'What did teacher say?'

A bell came ringing through the wall as the shop door opened.

'He said it's because of alienation.'

'Good word, that.'

'Peer-group pressure, and the need to bond.'

'You swallow the textbook?'

'Is it right, though, Billy?'

He spread his legs, leaned back in the chair.

'What d'you reckon, sweetheart?'

She thought about it for a moment.

'I think you just like hitting people.'

The Billy grin.

'You on the till, are you?'

'Might be,' she said.

'Cause you better get back, then.'

'You think so, do you?'

'Better not keep the punters waiting.'

She tossed her hair.

'I never keep them waiting, Billy. Wouldn't do that, see. Not to a punter.'

And she gave him the benefit of her schoolgirl smile, edged slowly out and pulled the door shut behind her. Billy stared across the desk.

'You want to watch her, Albert.'

'Don't I know it.'

Billy sometimes wondered what would happen if the old man died, and the girl took over. He'd never collected from a tart before, and he wondered what he'd have to do if she started proving troublesome. He had his standards, and he wasn't one for hitting women, unless they really asked for it. Whatever they might say, he did his best to let them be. But if they begged for it, if their names were Donna bitch and they went down on their knees and begged, he was always ready to do his duty, he'd do his best to be obliging.

A sudden recollection of an unploughed field in Hertfordshire. The field, the mist, the grinning boys. The slap of skinhead palm on tender girly cheek. The reddening face, the swelling mouth. He found the vision immensely pleasing and reached for some strawberry sponge. Fragility, he told himself. Can't beat it.

'Turned out nice,' Albert murmured. 'Bit of winter sun, eh? Can't be bad, Bill, can it.'

'Billy.'

'Can't be bad, Billy, can it.'

'No.'

The shopkeeper's eyes were running again. Every winter they started to water, and every summer the tear ducts dried up. Flood and drought, the skinhead realized. Like in the Bible. He sipped his tea. The steam was flowing up his face, and his feet were sweating inside his boots. It worried him, when that occurred. He'd read this article on jungle warfare, how squaddies got infected feet. Wet-foot, as the paper called it. They got a kind of fungus between their toes, and he hated things like that. You ended up lying flat on your back, stuffed with drugs and completely helpless. And all those nurses, prodding with their nursey hands. He put the mug down and eyed the money.

'Doesn't look like much there, Albert. Recession's over, or haven't you heard?'

'I got overheads, haven't I.'

Billy sighed.

'We've all got those.'

Albert spooned some sugar into his cup.

'There's some boys,' he muttered, 'little bastards.'

'What boys, Albert?'

The man stirred his tea, lowered his voice.

'Hooligan types, if you know what I mean.'

The skinhead nodded. He knew what he meant.

'I mean they walk right in and help themselves.'

'It's a cash-and-carry. You got a sign outside.'

'But they're all carry, aren't they. Not a lot of cash, see?'

'How much they taking?'

'Varies.'

'Roughly.'

He narrowed his eyes.

'About ninety, I reckon.'

'A month?'

'A week.' Albert shook his head. 'I mean ninety quid a fucking *week*. I got a problem, here. You know what I'm saying?'

'I hear you, Albert, but what can I do? It's the area, see. It's a rough old place. You ought to set up somewhere nice, somewhere where you won't get hassle.'

Albert shrugged.

'Like where?'

'Like . . .'

Billy dredged his brain for images of niceness and gentility. The names of suburbs loomed inside his head, while market towns enticed him with their wholesomeness. Finally he muttered:

'Cheltenham.'

'But I'm here, son, aren't I. My business is here, and my problem is here, and I'm meant to be getting protection, see.'

The skinhead lifted a warning finger.

'You complaining?'

'I'm not complaining. Just losing money.'

Billy shrugged.

'Money isn't everything.'

Albert stared, mid-swallow.

'You made a joke, there, Billy.'

'Did I?'

'You're a skinhead, son, and you made a joke.'

Billy nodded.

'I guess I did.'

Albert plucked a biscuit from the plate and crammed it into his mouth. Wholemeal crumbs cascaded down his shirt.

'I need a *presence*, see. Something to scare the bleeders off.'

Billy pondered.

'Get a dog.'

The old boy sighed. He'd try again.

'So tell me this, OK? I got one simple question, and I'd like you to answer it.'

'Be a pleasure, Albert.'

He settled back expectantly.

'Why do I pay you?'

'Sorry?'

'I mean I pay protection, right?'

'Right.'

'And I've got a problem, right?'

'Right.'

'And you don't want to sort it. Right?'

'Right.'

'So why am I paying you?'

Billy furrowed his brow, for it was an interesting point. He mulled it over in his Billy brain. Albert leaned forward.

'I mean who, exactly, are you protecting me *from*?'

The bashful, Billy face as he remembered.

'From me and Merv and Henry, Albert.'

Of course, he thought. Stands to reason.

'From us, old mate.'

And he picked up his mug and slowly smiled, all soft pink cheeks and cupid lips.

25

'You know something?'

She was staring out of the window.

'We missed the ending.'

'What ending?'

'The movie,' she said. 'We don't know what happened.'

'Right,' he grunted.

He took out a fresh pack of cigs and slowly unpeeled the cellophane.

'Shame, that.'

Two hours after Mervyn, and they're parked and waiting down Lambeth Road. The chill was leaking through the glass, her breath condensing in the air. Mid-afternoon, and a dankly shining London day, bright with noise and leaden with fumes. Packed double-deckers spewing out diesel, fluorescent labourers digging up the road. A gang of lumpy schoolgirls lurking on the corner, eating cheese-and-onion crisps and aching for a ruck. A raucous, blaring kind of day that makes you feel alive. The stench of it, the pure and perfect reek. The sort of day that makes your finger start to quiver and your head begin to burst, that makes you want to turn to someone close to you and let him glimpse your soul.

'How d'you want to die, Joey?'

He considered for a moment.

'I don't want to.'

'That's where we differ.'

'I know.'

'Because I've been planning my own departure like other girlies plan their weddings. Down to the last detail, see, because I don't want to mess up on my big day. Even thinking about it gives me pleasure, and I like a bit of pleasure, Joe. Just now and then. I'm not averse to being pleasured, on occasion.'

He lit a cigarette and took a thoughtful drag.

'Do you think that's normal?'

'I never said I was normal, Joey. Never made outrageous claims like that.'

When she died, she thought, she'd like to die in London. Let them sentence her and string her up. Let them hang her by her thin and fragile neck, she wouldn't mind. She knows you've got to keep them happy, give the punters what they want. Let the low-life come and gawp, let them watch her slowly turning in the air, gently swaying in the breeze. Let them pick up snotty toddlers so they'd have a better view. See, they'd say, nodding at the unlamented, pointing at the dear departed. See what happens, when you're bad.

She pictured the glorious scene, the public extinction of her perfumed self. Trafalgar Square on a Saturday night. The velvet sky, the lions keeping guard, the double row of coppers holding back the pressing crowd, penning in the urgent throng.

The whiff of frying burger to keep the hunger pangs at bay. The TV arc lights blazing down. The human slime of tabloid hacks. The silent executioner. Her last and final words, the parting thoughts she'd offer to humanity. The hood, the rope, the sudden loss of wood beneath her feet.

A millisecond's dangling pain and terror.

And then the bliss of nothingness. Then rest in peace, then fuck them all, then Donna bitch in paradise.

'Here we go,' Joe said.

He stuck the fag between his lips and turned the key. The engine shuddered into life.

She peered through the tinted windscreen, and there was a sudden tightness in her chest, a moment of contraction, a passing recollection of an empty field in Hertfordshire, of mud in her face and earth in her mouth and hearing the cunt word, over and over. She watched him coming striding out. He had a jaunty kind of look, a look of skinhead satisfaction, all jeans and polished ankle-boots. Sunlight bouncing off his head, and that smile on his face, that Billy grin.

'Who's the other guy?'

'What guy?'

'The one in the cardi.'

'That's Albert.'

'What's Albert like then?'

Joe pushed the gear-stick into first and released the hand-brake. He held the clutch at biting point.

'He's a bit like me.'

They watched as Billy said goodbye. He patted Albert's greying head and punched him lightly on the chin. Nothing nasty, nice and friendly. Then he turned around and climbed into his car. (Souped-up BMW. A very Billy kind of car.) The driver's window sliding down, and an elbow resting on the sill. Pause to scratch the razored scalp, and he was pulling sharply out, forcing a path into the line of vehicles.

She clipped on the seatbelt. Took his time, she thought, but she's not complaining. All things come to she who waits, and the boy was on his way.

Joe eased his foot off the clutch and edged out into the traffic.

'You OK?'

'Yeah I'm OK. Are you OK?'

'I'm fine.'

Not long now, she thought. She settled back against the headrest. Not too long, she told herself. They were heading up to Waterloo. Going slowly, crawling more than coasting. She watched the endless sprawl of shops unfolding through the window. She had a tension in her gut, the sort of feeling she always got when she crossed the river. A vaguely anxious feeling, for she's what they call a northern girl. South London, she was thinking, you can keep it.

They'd switched the car the day before. Dumped the Capri near Maida Vale, and picked up an Opel Manta. Two-and-a-half litres and walnut trim, and seats that cupped you where you liked it best. Metallic black, and so hot it would scald you, so freshly stolen you'd ache with envy.

Felt good though, driving out of Lambeth in someone's well-kept motor. Let no-one say it doesn't feel good. You get a sort of tingle down your spine, because you're driving something decent, you're feeling like you matter. And Joe had done it, because he cared. She just pointed to the one she wanted, and in he went.

She likes that type of man. She likes the type who'll be standing by her side in Maida Vale, and she'll point at what she wants and say: 'That one'll do,' and he'll cross the road and be inside in thirteen seconds, he'll slip inside and wire it while she's waiting. Then – bang! – you're up and running, engine throbbing. In, and grin, and off you go.

They kept about five cars back. They didn't want to get too close, if they could possibly avoid it. They didn't want to shove themselves on top of him. They maintained their distance, and kept their eyes on the small blue cloud that was pumping from his twin exhaust. Have to tell him, she concluded. Got to have a word in Billy's shell-like. Have to let him know he's fouling up the atmosphere.

Waterloo Bridge, then Covent Garden, and cruising past the British Museum. Carry on up to Euston Road, and they're almost on her morning route, which train of thought afforded her a glow of quiet contentment. (The pale grey suit, the Chelsea boots . . .) It suddenly seemed an age ago, the Mervyn thing. He'd been, and gone, and was no more, and not a whiff remained. The gentle Donna smile as she remembers. Such a lad, she thought. Such a naughty boy.

When she realized they were passing Malet Street, she sat a little straighter in her seat, for she's always had a great respect for learning, being fairly erudite herself. She's always got a book or two beside her bed. She's always starting books. Doesn't often finish them, but she always likes to start. The rain was spitting down, though nothing too dramatic. A few half-hearted drops that bounced onto the bonnet and spattered in the road. But even so, the passers-by were looking grim. Academics trudging home, foreign students plotting coups, all the mulch and detritus of a windswept Russell Square.

Joe watched the BMW go racing on ahead.

'Bastard's really belting. Giving it some throttle.'

He changed down to third, cutting in front of a Telecom van. Nearly clipped it, which nearly gave her stress. She glanced at him, but his face was impassive. Rigid mouth in a thin, tight line, the knuckles white on the steering wheel. Quietly and politely imploding.

They followed their boy down the underpass and out the

other end. A bit of London tunnel to simplify the ride. Short and sweet, past Euston Square. You've hardly gone in and you've come out again, and then you're cruising along into Marylebone Road, feeling good because it's almost done. But still the core of doubt, the girly hesitation.

'What if someone sees?'

'Doesn't work like that.'

'But if they do . . .'

'They won't believe it.'

'How do you know?' she persisted.

'Because I know.'

Two hundred yards past Madame Tussaud's, and the skinhead moved over into the left-hand lane. Joe checked the wing mirror and nudged the wheel.

'He's going for the turn-off.'

He pulled into Billy's line of traffic. They were four cars behind. Her bag felt heavy in her lap.

'At the fork,' he murmured. 'Right . . . ?'

Three cars behind.

'Right.'

Her reply so soft she almost couldn't hear it, and she felt her heart, her tiny, Donna heart, begin to thump inside her chest. The windscreen was steaming up, almost sweating with excitement. She watched his hand reach out and flick on the demister. She felt lucid, connected, as if all the threads had been pulled together. A perfect London day, with the sunlight shafting down, the very air electric, and she's plugged in, switched on, tooled up. Speed and light and retribution.

She flipped down the sunshield, checked her face in the mirror. All is vanity, she didn't quite remind herself, as she passed her tongue over rose-red lips. She slipped on a pair of shades, and gazed at her reflection. The bitch, she thought, the luscious bitch. Joe tensing in his seat.

'You ready, babe . . . ?'

Two cars behind. Coming up to Lisson Grove. She slipped her hand inside the bag and closed her fingers round the grip.

'Yeah,' she breathed. 'Been ready all my life.'

Four hundred yards from the flyover. One car behind. She lifted out the automatic. Kept it pointing down, below the sill. A chic little matt-black shooter. A very girly kind of gun. The sunlight shafting down, the very air electric, and she's switched on, plugged in, tooled up. Speed and light and retribution.

Billy quite oblivious, his shaven head absorbed in random Billy thoughts.

She kept her eyes on the back of his car, focused on the blue-grey cloud that mushroomed from the chassis. Forty feet behind him. Her mouth felt dry. She pressed a button. The window slid down. Air came scudding against her face. Joe cleared his throat.

'Just say the word . . .'

The sunlight shafting down. Speed and light and retribution.

'Now, Joe, baby. Do it now . . .'

He palmed the gear-stick into second and floored the pedal. The car swerved forward. Everything fluid, everything polished. He pulled alongside the BMW. The flyover looming up ahead, and Joe held it steady, keeping them parallel. She twisted in her seat, gripped the pistol double-handed.

So near they were, she could have reached across and touched him, could have stroked his downy cheek and helped him understand that life is unpredictable and bad boys are expendable. He was staring straight ahead, completely unaware, and she's willing him to look across, for she likes her bit of human contact, she likes some interaction. So come on, darling, come on, sweetheart . . .

'Do it, babe.'

'He's got to see it.'

'Just do it, will you?'

But she's paralysed with pleasure. It's eighty yards before the turn-off, and she's savouring the moment. Joe cursed his unforgiving gods and touched the horn. Billy glanced across. A brief, untroubled driver's glance. All he saw was some slag in a car, with a bright red mouth and mirror shades. His bland, unworried skinhead face. No hint of recognition.

So she spread her lips and smiled at him. Her special smile. Her hello-fuckhead sort of smile. Sunlight shafting down, the very air electric. And then a sudden tightness in her chest. A moment of contraction. A putrid recollection of an empty field in Hertfordshire . . .

But she's plugged in, switched on, tooled up. Speed and light and retribution. She blows the boy a silent kiss and her finger pulls the trigger. Three flawless rounds come shooting out, and she's saying the cunt word, over and over.

26

Joe pressed the buzzer and held it down. Getting dark, the wind licking at his face.

'You sure about this?'

He hunched into his jacket.

'Cause if you're not entirely positive . . .'

She pulled a sliver of green paint off the door-jamb.

'Might as well.' She shrugged. 'I mean it's something to do, isn't it.'

He grunted quietly and took his finger off the button. She was beginning to spoil his afternoon. Not massively, but just enough.

'But why now, sweetheart? Why when we're busy?'

'Because I like a bit of variety, Joe. That's why.'

She pushed in front of him and knocked on the door. She'd changed in the car, and was wearing what she termed her Billy outfit: lilac blouson jacket, a pair of tight-cut jeans, and high-heeled, black-suede ankle-boots. Looking pretty good, she thought, in a slaggy sort of way. She knocked again, for she likes to make an entrance. She likes to make her presence felt.

'No-one in,' he muttered.

'You wish.'

He stared down at the ground, scuffed a toe against the doorstep. A sense of creeping dread had engulfed him ever since she'd suggested this, and the more he thought about it, the more it seemed a reckless thing to do.

'Look,' he said quietly, 'if they're there – which doesn't seem likely – we just go in, do the business, and come out, right?'

'Sure, Joe.'

'I mean we won't stay long, OK?'

'Course not.'

She touched him lightly on the arm, soothed him with her tender smile. So good she was. So comforting. So milk of human kindness.

'We'll do the necessary,' she promised, 'and then we'll leave.'

''Cause it's not in the plan, is it?'

'I know it's not, but we've got to stay loose, see, got to be flexible.'

She rapped her knuckles on the door, still feeling high. An hour or so after the freeway thing and the film was spooling through her head, unfolding in her brain. The automatic in her hand and London gusting through the window. Flyover looming straight ahead, and they're gliding up beside him. Smooth and fluid, torpedo in the water. Pause for solemn contemplation, wait to savour what was coming . . . then sunlight on her skin, and the road like molten silver, and the unbelieving Billy face exploding.

'We could even have tea,' she suggested, 'if they're around.'

'You hungry, then?'

'Bit peckish.'

He watched her bang on the door, heard it echo down the road.

'You're making a noise,' he muttered.

'Thought you liked it, when I did that.'

'Not me, darling.'

He pressed his lips against her neck.

'You must be thinking of someone else.'

She considered the possibility.

'Yeah,' she murmured. 'Guess I must.'

A finger of mist curled inside the porch. Joe shivered slightly. Be foggy later. He could smell it in the air, that barren smell of late November. He pushed back his sleeve and squinted at his watch.

'We'd better shift,' he said. 'They're not there, anyway.'

She held her breath and listened.

'I reckon they are.'

With perfect timing, and as if on cue, indistinct sounds came wafting from inside, a kind of slippered shuffle that gradually grew louder as it moved towards them down the hallway. Joe pulled down his cuffs and cleared his throat. The shuffling sound had halted just behind the door, and it dawned on him, with a sudden, lurching horror, that there were certain things in life which couldn't be avoided. A wave of curdled panic washed over him, and for a single, terrifying second he thought he might collapse.

'In and out,' he hissed. 'Right?'

They heard the eternal, urban sound of bolts being drawn back, locks being turned, a security chain slotted into place. The door opened a couple of inches and a watery blue eye, slightly myopic, peered through the gap. Thinning grey hair, the eyebrow plucked to nothing, but a soft and gentle voice, a voice like Joey's voice.

'Hello, baby.'

Oh precious, precious moment.

'Hello, mum.'

27

Henry swivelled slowly in the chair, describing semicircles in the dusk. He found the motion vaguely calming, and he wanted to be calm. There was a pulsing in his head, and a burning in his gut, and he needed, fairly badly, to be calm.

The curtains were hanging slightly open, and a grubby, yellow light leaked in from the street. He stared at the shadows on the desk. Almost looked like they were moving. Almost seemed like something crawling in the gloom. He placed his thumb and middle finger on the bridge of his nose. His brain felt gummy with exhaustion. Time he had a rest. Too old for this, he told himself. More a young man's game. More a game for brave young bloods. Should have packed his bags and headed off to Spain, cashed in his chips and gone off to the Costa. Got a bit of sunshine on his bones. Not fair, he thought, not fucking fair.

He shut his eyes and cocked his head, trying hard to concentrate. The phone was clamped to his ear. He was listening intently.

'Tell me again.'

He gently kneaded his temples.

'I know that, son. Now I want it again.'

He heard the voice come hissing down the line, reluctantly going over the story. Savouring, despite itself, the juicy bits. The phone was welded to his ear, and he could scarcely believe what he was hearing. It was like listening to the wireless, he thought, like hearing a play on Radio Four, some piece of far-fetched make-believe that slips down with the cocoa.

A fairy tale for city folk: first they did this, and then they did that. First the cinema, then the freeway. First the neck-job, then the drive-by. He felt a stab of sentimental envy, for he'd been young once, he'd done that. Gone out in a rage and settled all his debts. And once you started, you didn't want to stop. Like eating walnut whips, he mused. Just the one was never quite enough.

'You got a firm ID yet?'

He scratched the back of his head.

'Course you can. Fucking told me everything else . . . Yeah, yeah, you got my word . . . Bloke and a tart? That what they reckon? . . . Nah. Got no idea, mate . . . On my mother's life, may she rest in peace . . . I would if I could, believe me.'

He opened his eyes.

'Look, no-one's taping, all right?'

He listened patiently.

'I know it's a risk . . . Yeah, I know you are. And don't think I don't appreciate it, because I don't.'

He laughed softly. What a wag, he thought. Ought to be on the telly.

'You know me, pal, only kidding. You're on a bonus, after

this . . . Yeah, mate. You've done good.'

Bit of stroking he reflected. Never went amiss.

'But I'll tell you something, right? Your lot better get their finger out, cause we don't want crap like this, old son. Cause this is London, see, not fucking Manchester. We don't want girlies getting shooters. Just catch her quick, you hear? Brick her up in some hole in the wall, and give her a flick knife to play with.'

The hissing down the wire. Giving him a headache.

'Yeah, yeah . . . Right . . . You're doing good. Like I said, it's appreciated . . . No, I mean that.'

Enough, he thought, the other man's voice beginning to grate. He had things to do now. There were plans to lay, plots to hatch. Provisions which needed to be made. All of it swirling through his brain, coagulating in his head. Milk drink first, he told himself. Coat his stomach with something gentle, before he started.

'Look, relax, OK? You're in a call box, nothing can happen. Stay cool, all right? . . . No, listen, I'm telling you. It won't be traced.'

A sudden spasm in his belly.

'So fuck your job. You know what I'm saying? Just fuck it, right?'

He cut the connection. Silence in the room. Getting dark, the street light growing stronger. He flicked on the desk lamp and the knowledge hit him. It slammed him hard in his ravaged gut.

My lads, he realized. They've done my lads . . .

28

'He was a lovely baby,' Beryl remarked. 'Slept all night. Quite uncomplaining.'

She began to carve the chocolate cake. They were sitting in the parlour of a terraced house in Acton Town. Matching three-piece suite and telly from the rental firm. The faint yet pleasing odour of suburbia.

'Didn't like stress though,' she was moved to add. 'Never much cared for aggravation.'

Laid out the slices on a floral plate.

'Wants a nice, quiet life, I've always thought.'

The fond, indulgent smile.

'He's a simple soul.'

She poured out the tea.

'But big and strong, have you noticed that, dear? He's a strapping young lad.'

She dropped two sugars into her cup.

'Didn't get weaned till he was thirty months.'

A sympathetic Donna murmur.

'Must have been distressing for you.'

'It was, dear, frankly.'

A sip of milky tea.

'Specially for the nipples, if I recall correctly.'

Joe shut his eyes and quietly shuddered. It can't last long, he told himself. Be over soon, he fantasized. A finger poked him in the ribs.

'Wake up, Jo-jo. Mustn't nod off . . .'

She was passing round the biscuits. He wouldn't say no to a macaroon.

'Where's dad?' he asked.

'The Dada's upstairs.'

She flicked her eyes towards the ceiling.

'He had to lie down.'

She lowered her voice to a confidential whisper.

'He's got his condition . . .'

'Oh.'

She nodded sadly and helped herself to a custard cream. A hush descended on the room, some brief yet brimming seconds when thoughts were focused on the Dada, then Joey said, for he liked to show an interest:

'How's the tum then, ma? Getting better, is it?'

'You mean my gallstone tum?'

'The very same.'

She bestowed on him a grateful smile. She swelled with validation.

'Healing nicely, as you're asking.'

She looked at her son expectantly.

'Like to see it, would you?'

'Another time, perhaps.'

'For mummy, Joey . . .'

'Fraid we've got to dash.'

She undid her blouse and rolled up her vest.

'Just a quickie, then. As you're only passing . . .'

There was a five-inch ridge of glossy flesh, salmon-pink and vertical.

'Had it done last month, up the Royal Free. A female ward. All girls together, which was how I liked it. Couldn't have stood it on a mixed-sex ward. You're in your nightie and all defenceless, and some pervert's leering while you sleep.'

She gazed at the scar almost tenderly.

'See that hole?'

'What hole?'

'Down there.'

She pointed at her side.

'That's where they had the tube,' she said. 'Drained out all the juices. Could have put a straw in, if I wanted.'

A regretful sigh.

'All gone now, though,' and she pulled down the vest, and did up the blouse.

Donna put her tea plate on the table.

'You're looking very well,' she said, 'considering.'

She picked up her bag.

'Isn't she, Joe?'

The unresponsive Joey gaze.

'Your mother, Joe. I said she's looking well.'

He nodded dumbly.

'She's got a very good skin.'

The mother smiled demurely at the girl.

'That's because of my sweet nature,' she said.

Joe gulped down his tea.

'I thought it was because you're a vegetarian.'

The mother swivelled her gaze towards him.

'That too.'

Joe stood and stretched.

'Have to go now, mum.'

'Can't you stay a bit more?'

'In a bit of a rush, see. Got to make a move.'

He helped his girly to her feet.

'You want a bit of cash, I've got some spare.'

'You keep it, Jo-Jo. Buy your lady something nice.'

She smiled at baby's girlfriend and imparted the secret of her existence.

'I've been teetering all my life,' she said. 'Been standing on the brink, you see.'

'But you haven't fallen . . .'

'No,' she conceded. 'But I've always teetered.'

They walked back out to the street door. A fleeting clasp of hands, and the niceties had been observed. They felt themselves relax, the tension leak away. Beryl hesitated, for a moment, then touched the young girl's arm. Tentative, half-doubtful.

'Take care of him,' she whispered. Thinning, grey hair, eyebrows plucked to nothing, but a soft and gentle voice, a voice like Joey's voice.

'Cherish him, my Joey-boy . . .'

29

The pan was simmering nicely now, giving off a milky smell. He shifted his weight on the stool. It was a pleasurable movement, for he liked to feel hard wood beneath his soft rump. It made him feel quite virtuous, to rest his fleshy peachiness on something hard and smooth.

The leather album lay open on the kitchen table. His cuttings album, the proof of what he was. Every time they wrote about him, he cut the snippet out and glued it in. Been collecting them for years, his passing mentions, his little bits of immortality. Subscribed to all the nationals, and sent his boys to pick up every local rag in town, in case it featured you-know-who, in case it carried something that he'd done, some tale of viciousness and random spite. Described a bone too soft to be believed, the kind that shouldn't be allowed, the sort suggestive of deficiencies in nourishment, the kind of bone that splintered when he breathed on it, that crumbled when he touched it.

It took him time to gather, though. Too much time, he sometimes thought. The slow collecting of the scraps of printed him, the short, truncated paragraphs describing what he'd done, the moist and swelling pain within his chest because they never mentioned who he was, they never named the one responsible. The Henryness of what was done was simply unrecorded. Always just a reference to what they called an 'unknown assailant'. That's me, he'd proudly tell himself. I do believe the one they mean is me.

There were companies that did that kind of thing, special firms which scoured the press for mentions of their clients. Only cost a grand or so a year, he'd heard. Sports stars used them. Movie types. Celebrities, and cunts like that. Paid to have their cuttings culled. But Henry had to do it all himself, go digging through the verbiage himself. He had to trawl through all the shit and filth, the rank and loathsome pages of humanity, the stink of all those stinking little lives, go wading through the mire, go crawling through the dung of other people's dreams, until he found the gem, the pearl, the cut and shining diamond of perfection: a paragraph of motiveless brutality, a hundred glistening words on him, and what he'd done to someone who deserved it.

A thick and much-thumbed scrapbook, what he liked to term the Book of Henry. He'd been saving the cuttings since he turned seventeen, a fresh young lad just out of Borstal, with a smile on his face and a cosh in his hand. He began to turn the pages, reading quickly, skimming through each glued-in story and moving on to the next. His gaze came to rest on a sliver of yellow newsprint. 'Random Assault', the headline stated, and underneath, in fading biro: 'East Ham Recorder, March '62.'

Big John, as he recalled. Big John from Bermondsey, with

the squinty eyes, the runny nose, and the very lippy mouth. Got out of line, and had to learn. You're nice to them, he thought, you're fucking nice and kind to them, and they take advantage, they always let you down.

A misty vision swam into his brain. An underpass in Shoreditch on a rainy Tuesday night, and he'd offered John a fag, given him a Player's Number One. The big man bending down, the scrape of match, the orange flame, and then an uppercut that landed on his jaw, the knee between the legs, the punching to the ground. Big John from Bermondsey. Been shafted, well and truly. Buggered up, completely. He'd gone right in, and poked around. He'd had a good look round. Had a butcher's, so to speak. Paid a visit and said hello. Passed the time of day. Henry sighed benignly. Oh youth, he thought. Oh happy days.

He poured out the boiling milk. East Ham, 1962. He raised the mug to his waiting lips. Steam curled damply round his face. That's me, he thought. That's what I am. The bloke who's waiting in the dark. The unknown fucking assailant. A sudden rush of self-regard, and the liquid lapped against his mouth as he began to suck the skin.

30

They took the Westway back to town, came bombing up the motorway and powered down past Ladbroke Grove. Foot down hard, headlights cutting through the darkness. Just him and her and a stolen car, and a bleak, beguiling London night, all drifting fog and desolation.

The sort of night, you weren't too careful you'd have a crash, you'd skid across the road and slam against a lorry. You'd be meditating on the fatman, planning how you'll say hello, and suddenly you've jerked the wheel, you've wrenched the leather steering wheel and crashed into the side. You'd be bombing back to town, lost in splendid contemplation, and the bits inside your head, the brainy bits, the sub- and hypothalamus, would gradually expand. They'd pulse and throb until, engorged with blood, they burst upon an unsuspecting world. So better be like Donna bitch, live in hope and stay alert. Better slide the window down, so the air comes gusting in, and the chill starts gnawing at your bones.

Joe flicked on the heater.

'Hope he's there.'

He turned the knob to maximum.

'Because he might be out.'

'He won't be out.'

'Might have been invited round for dinner.'

She pulled a face.

'You ever watch him eat?'

A memory of shining chins and dribble. Joe shut his eyes and quietly shuddered.

'Fair point,' he grunted.

They came off fast, and she hung a left into Edgware Road. Two in the morning and the place was buzzing, full of hip young things with time to kill. Hanging loose and looking cool. Like us, she thought, just young kids having fun. She nudged the car against the kerb.

'We pulling in?'

'Thought we'd get some ciggies, Joe. Bit of chocolate, sort of thing.'

He tugged open the ashtray, began counting butts.

'How many you smoking a day, these days?'

'Counting everything?'

'Totting it up.'

'Not many,' she muttered.

'How many's not many?'

She cut the engine.

'Twenty or so.'

'About a pack . . .'

'Yeah.' She shrugged. 'Roughly.'

'You saying it might be more?'

She took out her lipgloss.

'I'm saying I've got stress, Joe. That's what I'm saying.'

She dabbed some colour on her mouth.

'Yeah, well . . .' He slid the gun into his pocket, felt the comforting weight on his thigh. '. . . I don't believe in stress and stuff.'

She unclipped the seatbelt.

'That a fact?'

'It is.'

'Would have thought you might, after what happened.'

'Sorry?'

'The other day,' she said.

'What was that, then?'

'What they did,' she said. 'That thing they did.'

'Oh.'

The Donna bitch. He stared at the dashboard. Silence leaked into the car.

'We going in?' he murmured, finally.

The shop was an all-nighter, the kind of place that's crammed with booze, that's stuffed with wired-up, sleepless types, and always has a guard-dog by the counter. Blue-white glare reflected off the glass and bounced between the walls, and the floor was smeared with muck and water trailed in from the street. She wandered slowly round the aisles. She liked to take her time.

'What you getting?'

'Little bit of this,' she said. 'Little bit of that.'

'Some cigs and chocolate, right?'

'Don't rush me, Joe.'

'Cause I don't like waiting, see? There's one thing I can't bear it's hanging round while someone's shopping.'

'You starting, Joe?'

'I'm only saying.'

'Go say it in the car, you're feeling bored.'

'I just don't like waiting.'

'So fucking go, then.'

'Shall I?'

'Yeah.'

Joe shrugged. When she got like that, started mouthing off, he'd always rather leave. He went out into the street, felt the dampness seep into his bones. The fog was getting denser, climbing up the walls and congealing round the lamp-posts. He got back in the car and sat behind the wheel. The windows were beginning to ice up. He turned on the demister.

Be over soon, he thought. He took out a cigarette and placed it between his lips. Slope up Hampstead way, he thought, and they'd finish it, quite soon. He struck a match and held the yellow flame against the tip. Sucked the goodness into his lungs and blew it out in a long grey plume.

'Can't bear waiting,' he muttered quietly. 'Fucking loathe it, don't I.'

A rustle from behind. A whiff of milk and middle age.

'Funny you should say that, son . . .'

The four-inch blade against his neck.

'. . . cause so do I.'

31

It took them forty minutes or so to get from Edgware Road to Tufnell Park. Joe stayed down in second gear, because of the fog, and because of the knife. He was sitting rigid in the seat, trying not to move too much. If he shifted his weight when making a turn, the blade would gently cut his skin. There'd be a consciousness of pain, a sudden intimation of mortality. He focused on the road, watching tail-lights glow and disappear. There was a void inside his head, an empty, vacant feeling, a sense of things unravelling.

'You think she saw us?'

Henry, leaning forward. The fragrant tang of rotting gut.

'Cause it occurs to me she might have come out just as we were leaving, come running out the shop all loaded down with sweets and tampons, seen us shooting down the road.'

The soft, seductive fatman hiss.

'That's what I've been thinking, see, and it's a tantalizing thought.'

He moved the hand that held the knife, pressed it slightly closer.

'You listening, son?' Cause I'm talking, aren't I. Doing what's called making conversation.'

Joe was staring straight ahead. His thoughts were slowly clearing, brain kicking into gear. He couldn't see much road, just swirls of mist, a yard or so of broken lines. If he hadn't known the way, if he hadn't known the curves and bends of every street from Edgware Road to Tufnell Park, he might have panicked slightly. He might have lost his nerve and veered across the asphalt, shut his eyes and smashed against some overloaded skip. But he was Joey-boy the expert driver, and he knew what he was doing. Might have been a fatman in the rear and a blade against his throat, but the gun was weighing on his hip and he knew what he was doing.

They went from Baker Street to Camden, then up to Kentish Town and across to Tufnell Park. They looped around the football ground and doubled back towards the centre.

'Case we're being followed. Case girly's in a minicab, consumed with girly rage.'

The fatman chuckled softly. You could see he thought he was a wag. You could tell he liked himself, immensely.

'Now take a left,' he said. 'Straight on a bit. Another left. Good lad,' he breathed. 'You're a bright boy, Joe, like I've always said. Not quite as thick as you pretend. Go straight, go straight. Now slow a bit. Now *right*, son, that's it. Down the ramp.'

A municipal car park beneath the shops. You slid your pound inside the slot and in you went. The sort of place that's deserted after dark, so you could go there of an evening, park the car and do the business. Suburbia, don't knock it. Henry pressed his lips against Joe's ear and gave him his instructions. They circled down to the bottom level, pulled up near a lift. Joe cut the motor.

'So here we are, then,' Henry murmured. 'Alone at last.'

Neon light was sharding down, water dripping in a corner. Henry cocked his head and sniffed the air. There was a dank, familiar smell of engine oil and rubber. A pervy, car park kind of smell. He felt himself relaxing.

'Heard you were round your mum's Joe, you and little girly bitch. A major point in your favour, that, because I like a lad who loves his mum. Might pop round myself, sometime. Go round and introduce myself. Say: "Hello, Joey's mum." Might do it, if I'm passing. Have some tea and a currant bun. Be kind to her, that sort of thing.'

He smiled to himself, for he was feeling nice.

'My mum, Joe – may she rest in peace – she said I've got what she termed *foibles*. Because I like to be indulged a bit. I like to get my way.'

The milky breath on Joey's neck.

'I mean I take my pleasures where I find them, and I find them fairly often. You get my drift, son, course you do. Don't have to explain it, do I, eh? Not to you. Not soft and luscious Joey-boy.'

The blade against the throat.

'So me and you, son. Eh, Joe? Eh?'

Joe felt himself begin to shudder, the vomit churning through his belly. He heard his heartbeat marking time, like a rap song pounding in his ears. Not me, he thought, not that. The sweat came trickling down his back. He could smell the fear, could almost taste it. Concentrate, he told himself. Think, you cunt. Knife against your throat, loaded gun inside your pocket, and a voice that's seeping through your brain, saying: do it, Joe, just take a chance, just do it now . . .

And when he braced himself, when he pictured Donna in the dark and held his breath and braced himself, something must have flickered through his skin, perhaps his blood betrayed him. There was a sudden swish of movement, and then a blow that caught him from behind.

Like a brick against his skull. As if the bones exploded.

32

'They're good, these.'

Henry pulled out the clip and counted the rounds.

'Italian, see. From the land of vendetta.'

He slid the clip back in. Went in nice and smoothly, hardly made a sound.

'She fired three rounds, then. Quite a girl, eh? Have to watch my mouth when I catch up with her. Mustn't banter with Donna, must we, for she's not the bantering kind. Made a mess of Billy, I heard. Cause I've got my sources, Joe. Pals who phone me up and keep me posted, lads who keep me *au courant* with what transpires.'

He wiped the barrel on his sleeve.

'So we know why we're here, Joe, don't we. No beating round the bush, right? No need to go all . . . euphemistic. Because I like to call a spade a spade, I've always been an upfront sort of bloke.'

A sudden frown of doubt.

'You listening, Joe?'

He peered at the boy. He was propped against the Opel, one eye closed and turning blue. Henry bent down and tipped him forward slightly, to examine the back of his head. The blood seemed almost black. Like tar, he thought, disgustedly. He pushed him back against the wheel. He felt big with rage, engorged with loathing, the misanthropic urges getting stronger, deeper, ever warmer. He shoved the gun into the waistband of his trousers. There was a feeling of pleasurable discomfort as it chafed against his lower belly.

'What's that you wearing son? New jacket, is it? Bit of leather on your back? Can't be bad. I say it can't be bad. Made you feel a toff, I bet, walking round town with a jacket like that. Must have made you feel all right. Suits you, frankly. Bit of well-cut leather on a tough young lad like you. A mean and moody lad like you.'

He leaned towards him, lowered his voice.

'Except you're soft inside, so sweet inside. Like a summer peach, when you get inside.'

The fat and female Henry grin.

'Am I right, Joe?'

Cigar-stub clamped between his teeth.

'Tell me, Joey, am I right?'

Joe licked his lips and murmured 'fuck you' very softly. You'd have to strain to hear it. You'd have to tilt your head and cock an ear and concentrate, quite hard. Henry shook his head. He looked concerned.

'I do believe I've upset the boy. I do believe I have.'

The slow and drawn-out Henry sigh. He did his best, he

consoled himself, but it's always misinterpreted.

'How you keeping, anyway? Because you're looking a bit pale, if you don't mind me saying so. Looking slightly shattered, frankly.'

He narrowed his eyes.

'Been getting all your sleep, I hope. Been getting all your shut-eye, have we? I mean I hope she lets you get some rest. Because they're like that, aren't they? The girlies, Joe. Always making their girly demands. So I hope you're sleeping, cause there's nothing worse, I've always thought, than coping with life when you need some kip.'

He scratched his head.

'Or almost nothing.'

He bent down and grabbed the boy under the arms.

'Eight full hours I get. Just shut my eyes and off I go. Keeps me young and wholesome. Helps the juices flow.'

He began to heave him round.

'So I hope you're getting all you need, is what I'd like to say. Good for the skin, see. Nice and healthy. Help you keep that glow you've got.'

Grunting as he heaved.

'You know I like your glow.'

Heavy bastard, he was thinking. Hard fucking work, and no mistake.

'I mean we don't want Joey looking peaky. We like him when he's fresh and pretty.'

He was wheezing as he propped Joe up against the boot. Out of condition, he told himself. Been a while, though, hadn't it. Been a year or two since he'd done a solo. My boys, he thought. I need my boys. He squatted down on his haunches, tried to catch his breath.

'I feel I know you, Joe, because we've been what's termed as intimate. I think I understand the way you're feeling, and what you're in right now – the state, I mean – is what we call an existential crisis. You're hovering on the edge, old son, and I'm about to push you off.'

He spat the cigar-butt to the ground.

'You're too good for this world, so I'm sending you to the next.'

He grabbed Joe's shirt with his right hand, the belt with his left.

'I'm doing you a favour, you poor, benighted fuck.'

He flipped him over. A sudden vision of a verdant field, his bosom pals, a perfect day in Hertfordshire.

'Shame she's not here,' he mumbled, 'because I like it when she's watching.'

He heaved Joe forward a few inches. He hadn't done it this way before, so it'd be something new for both of them. Only problem, the boy might slip off, which would be unfortunate. Need someone to hold him, really. Need a Billy or a Merv to hold him steady, and they were gone, he sighed, the toe-rags.

He took Joe by the hair and lifted his head.

'You're shivering, son. Not looking too well. I should've brought a blanket, shouldn't I. Always use a duvet myself, but I guess it's too soft for a hard man like yourself.'

He carefully pulled open the jaw and pushed the broken mouth around the exhaust pipe.

'In we go,' he murmured. 'Gently does it.'

He moved Joe's arms and wrapped the hands around the pipe.

'Hold on, now. You hear?'

He stood up and stepped back. Might work, he thought. You never know.

'Just remember, son: you're not alone. I also suffer.'

He climbed into the driver's seat and closed the door. He'd brought some sweeties with him, to pass the time, and now he took one out and carefully unwrapped it. His mouth began to water. Not quite his favourites, but very nearly: full-cream toffee with banana whorls. And why not, he thought, as he popped the treat inside his mouth. A bit of what you fancy can't be bad.

He leaned against the headrest and slowly chewed, a feeling of mellow satisfaction spreading through him. I'm a lovable rogue, he told himself. Just got some foibles, he reflected. Just get impulsive, now and then, and he switched on the ignition, and the engine fired.

33

It was two days later when he got the call. A special package, they informed him, ready for delivery. Without a blemish, they were at pains to emphasize. Not a mark, and in perfect nick. So if he liked that type of thing, and was feeling somewhat partial, they'd fix a price and it was his.

Henry listened quietly. A sense of sublime contentment, of cosmic well-being, began flowing through him.

'Bring it round later,' he instructed. 'No, son, not here.'

He thought for a moment.

'Carlo's. You know it? Yeah. Bring it round the back, about half one.'

He replaced the receiver in the cradle. A car door banged across the street, teenage voices echoed in the darkness. He frowned at the wall. Yobbos, he thought, disgustedly. Hooligans, and vulgar types. He pushed back a cuff and glanced at his watch. Quarter past eleven, which meant a couple more hours to fill, couple more hours to prepare himself. Maybe have a bite before he went. Nothing too heavy, though. Nothing excessive. Scrambled eggs, or something. Perhaps a touch of cream.

He pushed himself away from the table and stood up, his cotton shirt clinging to his back. The sweat of anticipation, he told himself. The clammy moisture of desire. Better have a wash then, do the decent thing. Couldn't hurt, he told himself. He climbed the steps to the second floor, went into the bathroom and turned on the taps. Steaming water thundered down as he got undressed. Least I don't smell, he thought, peeling off a dark grey sock. He poured out a capful of bubble bath and watched it begin to foam. Might be impulsive, he reflected, as he slid down into the tub, but least I don't pong.

It was pleasant while it lasted, but all good things must come to an end, one always has to pull the plug. After the soaking, the tender fondling, he was rather reluctant to get dressed again. Could always stay in, he thought. Just phone and cancel, get some kip. Have some cocoa and an early night, and leave the business till tomorrow. He heaved a sigh of lubricious sadness, for he'd never been one to shirk his duty, he always liked to do his bit. So he pulled on his pants and his thermal vest. The lavender shirt, as he was feeling rakish, and the loose-cut suit with the wide lapels.

The leather of the shoulder holster, which he'd bought in Romford, was worn and softened. It was very supple leather. He slipped it up his arm, pulled the band across his chest and slid the tongue through the metal buckle. At first, as he recalled, being made for 45s, it had been too large for his delicate rich man's weapon. But he'd taken it round to an obliging cobbler, and now the pistol slid in smoothly, fitted snugly, like he would with little girly.

He put on the jacket and admired his reflection, felt the comforting weight beneath his arm. He hadn't bothered with the snack, and was already feeling hungry, getting that sour taste, that empty-fatman-belly taste, in his mouth. Have some pasta, maybe, when he got there. Some tagliatelli carbonara. He slicked some Brylcreem through his hair and combed it back, then licked a finger and smoothed down an eyebrow. Looking good, he told himself. You're looking fucking good, old mate.

He stepped onto the porch and closed the door gently behind him. Mervyn's Daimler was parked on the drive. Just like a Jag, he told himself. Like a hairdresser's motor. He'd barely started walking towards it when the passenger door swung open. The fatman climbed inside, savouring the smell of wood and pigskin. He glanced at the driver. Eighteen-odd, and barely shaving.

'All right, son?'

The driver nodded. The new lad, on probation.

'Let's go then, shall we?'

The car pulled into the road, tyres hissing on the wet tarmac. Henry lit a cigarette, flicking the match out of the window. The boy switched on the wipers and fumbled in his pocket.

'OK if I smoke too?'

'No.'

'Sorry?'

'Just drive, son.'

He sensed the boy shrug, heard him switch on the radio. Techno music jabbed inside his brain. He watched the orange lamplight trickling by.

'Off,' he said softly.

'Boss?'

'Turn it off.'

He pulled on the fag and the tip glowed red, reflecting back at him in the glass. Rain came streaking down the windscreen.

I'm clean, he thought. I'm scrubbed and ready.

The boy changed down to third, sent them surging past a lorry. Henry waited quietly. He'd give the boy a couple of moments, pause to let him think it through. He'd wait a while, till the fag burned down, till his nails began to feel the heat. Because there's no point being hasty, unless you really have to. No point acting prematurely. So he stared into the dark, a loaded gun beneath his arm and techno throbbing through his skull. Come on sunshine, be obliging. They flashed past Angel, heading up to Dalston. A final burst inside his head, and the noise was suddenly cut.

The pure, unfettered sound of silence.

'Good lad,' he murmured.

He spread his legs.

'We'll get on fine.'

34

There was only Carlo, when they got there, and he didn't look well. He had an agitated look, when you really looked. Henry punched him lightly on the shoulder.

'Everyone gone home then, have they?'

He stepped inside the empty restaurant.

'All packed up, and fucked off home?'

Carlo pulled down the blind and bolted the door.

'I closed up early,' he mumbled. 'After you called. Thought you'd prefer to keep it private.'

Henry nodded. The Henry smile.

'Keep what private?'

Pause for half a beat. Carlo treading water.

'Your dinner, Henry. Thought you wouldn't want to be disturbed.'

'That was very thoughtful of you.'

The fatman walked over to the corner table, motioning the boy to sit down opposite.

'You got anything in the oven?'

Carlo shook his head.

'We had some pigeon breast, before.'

'I like a bit of breast.'

'All gone, now, I'm afraid.'

'Punters like it, did they?'

'They loved it, Henry.'

'I'll bet they did, the bastards.'

Henry sighed, for he quite liked pigeon. It was a Henry kind of dish.

'Do me a steak, then.'

'How d'you want it?'

'As it comes.'

He took out his handkerchief and wiped his nose. Catching a chill, he thought. Shouldn't have had that sodding bath.

'Who's in the kitchen?'

'Just me, Henry. No problem.'

'I know that, Carlo. That's why I come here, see? Cause there's never any problem.'

The fatman moved the salt so it was next to the pepper, and flicked a breadcrumb to the floor.

'So better get cooking, then, if I was you. Better put your pinny on and do the business.'

He shoved the hanky back in his trousers. Glanced at the boy.

'What's your name, son? Oswald, is it?'

'Oscar.'

Henry nodded.

'Good name, that. Quite classy, really.'

The fatman drummed his fingers on the table and looked

around. Mellow light and polished wood. He almost felt at home.

'I like this place,' he muttered. 'Know what I mean?'

He undid his collar and loosened his tie, his fingers brushing the fleshy neck. The skin felt moist, for he was quietly sweating. Glowing with contentment. Be over soon, he thought. Be finished, well and truly.

The thick-cut fillet was medium rare, and when he cut it with his knife pink juice oozed out and slowly encircled the sauté potatoes. Nice bit of beef that, he told himself, cause he needed his protein. Helping of runner beans on the side, some pan-fried onions for character. There was a decent Bordeaux, to aid his digestion, while something classical came floating from the speakers. He put a chunk of steak inside his mouth and began to chew. The pleasing slap of lip on lip.

'I mean it's not a bad life, is it?'

He swallowed.

'Not fucking brilliant, but not too bad.'

He looked up at the young apprentice, the trainee driver, his dinner companion for the evening. Oscar blushed and moved his hand away from his face.

'What you doing there, son?'

'Nothing.'

Henry put down his fork.

'You picking your nose?'

'No.'

'You sure about that?'

'Course I'm sure.'

'Cause I could have sworn I saw your finger up your nose.'

Oscar shrugged.

'Just scratching, boss.'

'Inside the nostril?'

The boy wiped his finger on a napkin.

'Had an itch,' he shrugged. 'That's all.'

Henry looked at him. Bleak, unblinking eyes.

'Well I got news for you. You scratch an itch that's up your nostril, you're what we term a nosepicker, in the trade. And they never told me, did they, when I took you on. They never said: "Nice lad, Oswald, but he picks his nose." Didn't let me know upfront, so I could take precautions, see? Remember not to watch you while I eat my fucking *dinner*.'

He shoved the plate away in disgust. Oscar's gaze was focused on the steak.

'You leaving that?'

'You being funny?'

'I'm only asking.'

The fatman glared.

'Well fucking don't, right? Just keep it buttoned.'

His stomach was starting to churn, and he shoved a fag between his lips. He had a sudden vision of Merv and Billy, and for a second or two he almost missed them, he felt almost nostalgic. But they'd gone and left him and he was all alone, with acid forming in his gut and a tosspot for a driver. He shook his head and sucked on the fag. Not fair, he thought. Not fucking fair.

Footsteps sounded from behind the wall.

'Boss . . . ?'

The fatman swivelled round. Pushing through the kitchen door, with Carlo sweating close behind, came the Limehouse twins, two big, strong boys with shoulder pads. And tightly held between them, if he wasn't too much mistaken, permed and tinted and soft as chiffon, with tape stuck down on the ruby mouth, and thumbs tied together, in case she got fretful . . .

He felt himself go calm again, for all things come to him who waits. I'm clean, he thought. I'm scrubbed and ready.

'Hello, sweetheart.'

The warmth in the groin.

'Glad you dropped by.'

35

They stood in the yard behind the restaurant. Hardly room to move, for the ground was thick with empty crates, awash with plastic bin bags. A forty-watt bulb was jutting from the wall, throwing a dim, orange light over the wet brickwork. Half a mile away the night train was rumbling through Hackney. Be over soon, he told himself. Be finished, fairly soon. He glanced at the bruising on her chin.

'Thought you said without a blemish.'

The twins were wearing their velvet jackets, one in grey and one in blue. The grey one shrugged.

'She got lippy, Henry. Wasn't our fault.'

'Not a mark, you said . . .'

'We meant "more or less".'

Oscar groaned, an eruption of damply yearning breath that floated lazily into the night. He held her firmly by the arm, was eyeing her like she already belonged.

'Don't even think it,' Henry murmured.

'Think what, boss?'

'A bit of breaking and entering, son. Don't get ideas above your station.'

'I'm only looking.'

'Looking's fine. I don't mind looking. But I don't like leering. I don't like touching.'

The rain had almost petered out. Just a few soft drops, a residual spray. The wind came scudding through London Fields and bit into his skin. Alive, he thought, and feeling good, for he hugged inside himself the sure and certain knowledge that while Mervyn nearly got her, and Joe had gone and lost her, and Billy fell before her, later on tonight, most probably against her will, face down on some garage floor, he, and he alone, would be the one to have the vengeance-girl.

He turned to the Limehouse boys.

'Two thousand, right?'

He shoved a hand in his pocket and pulled out a wad of cash. Unused twenties, from the machine. He weighed the banknotes in his palm, the sum he'd agreed for his favourite slut.

'But is it a bargain, I ask myself?'

'Depends what you want it for.'

'That's very true.'

He peeled off notes and counted them over. He liked the feeling of money in his hands. Even when he paid it out, he got a sense of validation, of being someone who could buy the things he needed, who could lift the phone and say, Could you find my slag? Could you do it, please? Cause I'd be obliged. So he's feeling good, all things considered. He's feeling like a Henry should.

'You search her, lads?'

'First thing we did.'

'That right?' he said. 'What's the second thing, then?'

And he grinned at them, because he's only joking. He knew they wouldn't sniff around his package, try to poke their Limehouse fingers in its soft and tender places. Whatever they'd do, they wouldn't do that. They had their standards, after all, their prissy, gangster protocol.

'Where d'you find it, anyway?'

The blue twin smiled.

'Just wandering round.'

There was a final spattering of wind-blown rain as the last few banknotes were handed over. Time to shift, Henry thought. Time to make a move. He wouldn't want it getting soggy.

'Guess there's nothing much to say now, gents, except thank you kindly, and goodnight.'

And they all shook hands, for they were decent blokes.

36

'You got the locks on, son?'

He pushed his head forward between the two front seats and pointed at the dashboard. Oscar's finger hovered above a silver button. Henry nodded.

'That one, yeah.'

He settled back into the contoured seat and glanced at his watch. Twenty past three, and he needed his kip. If he stayed up too late his ticker started thumping, he'd get his palpitations. Because of her, the selfish cow. She was bad for his health. Infectious, really. A sort of germ, in human form. He turned his head and gazed at her. She was sitting in the corner, staring out of the smoked-glass window. She looked detached, he thought, like she was somewhere else. As if she didn't care, as if he didn't matter.

Oscar started the engine.

'We going home?'

The fatman thought it over.

'Eventually.'

He examined his nails. They were very white, he told himself. Very lovely.

'Thought we'd go for a spin first, Oswald. Have a little ride.'

He considered various options, and came to his decision.

'Leytonstone, why don't we.'

The driver pushed the gear-stick into second, and they jerked away from the kerb.

'Have to check the fuel tank,' he murmured. 'Something with the cable, boss. Got to sort it, case the engine cuts out.'

A languid movement of the fatman hand.

'Later, son. After we've finished.'

He smiled at the girl.

'D'you like my motor?'

Prodding her gently in the side.

'It's Mervyn's, see.'

She went on staring out the window. The bitch, he thought. The luscious bitch.

'Talk to me, sweetheart. I'm a lonely guy.'

He leaned towards her and yanked off the tape, and a stifled moan, a reluctant confession of pain, escaped her lips. That's more like it, he told himself. Always nice when they respond.

'So here we are again,' he said. 'Having one of our chats, our tête-à-têtes.'

The limo went cruising down the road, slicing through the urban sprawl round Homerton.

'I been reading about girls like you,' he said. 'Rough little girls who like causing bother. Been reading these articles in some very posh papers. And I know I shouldn't believe what they say, but sometimes I just can't help it, can I? They can't *all* be wrong, I tell myself. Not educated people, using lots of big words. Medical people, if you follow my drift. Men who specialize in your kind of problem. Diseases of the brain, my love. Abnormalities of the mental area. Cause when men like them say that girls like you need treating, who am I to argue?'

He slapped her round the mouth.

'You listening, precious? Cause I'm talking, see? So be a good girl and fucking look at me, right?'

Oscar sucked in his breath. He flicked a glance into the rearview mirror, then put his foot down hard and powered on through Leyton. He liked his new job enormously.

The fatman watched her turn her head. A trickle of darkness was edging down her chin. She fixed her gaze on his face, as if trying to memorize its features, as if she'd never really seen them before, she'd never really noticed them, and now was her final chance. A sound emerged from the back of her throat, as though she'd forgotten how to speak, she'd forgotten how to form the words.

'You say something, sweetheart?'

The fatman concern.

'Spit it out, darling. Don't be shy.'

Her mouth sagged open.

'What happened . . .'

She moved her lips.

'. . . to Joe?'

He felt himself relax, the tension leak away. His gut felt calm, his scrotum warm. His blood slowed down to a sullen throb of pleasure.

'I happened, didn't I.'

He took out his fags. It was a moment to savour, and it called for tobacco. He tapped the pack and offered the girl. No point being churlish, he thought. No point being stingy. Even lit it for her, being a true-blue gent, and watched her drag the muck and tar inside.

'It's very sad,' he added, 'but such is life.'

He lit one for himself, then placed the pack and matches in her lap. He was feeling in a generous mood, and ciggies wouldn't kill her. Whatever put her in her grave, it wouldn't be tobacco.

'You'll have to answer for it, though. What occurred. All the shit, and stuff. Because you caused it, really.'

He flicked a thin, grey turd of ash onto the carpet.

'You're what I'd call responsible, darling.'

He stared at the back of Oscar's neck. Rather closely shaved, he thought. Rather nineteen-fifties.

'Take us up to Epping, OK?'

'Sure, boss.'

Henry reached across and took her hand. He turned it over and examined the palm. He spread the fingers wide and gently touched the unlined skin.

'You been there, have you, up the forest? Our bit of country on the edge of London? Goes on for ever, if you're walking. You get lost in there, you're not too careful. Cause it's gigantic, darling . . .'

He placed her hand between his thighs.

'. . . it's fucking huge.'

They were speeding north: Woodford, Buckhurst, Loughton. The boy switched on the radio, surfing the channels till he found something bland. Henry tapped his foot.

'That's nice,' he murmured.

He leaned towards her and lowered his voice.

'Just us, the night, and the music, eh?'

Coming up to Debden, and the houses were getting fewer, the lights were getting scarcer, the sense that London's far behind. And suddenly, emerging from the gloom, spreading wart-like by the road, ten thousand half-bare trees. You could smell them in the car. Even sat in the back of a limousine, you could smell the trees in Epping Forest.

Oscar slowed and took a left.

'We stopping soon?'

'Just get in there, will you?'

The boy switched the lights to main beam, and drove on and in. He changed down to second, kept the revs down low. Moved from B-roads onto C-roads, then unmarked tracks. Tree trunks loomed and passed, while leafless branches slithered across the roof.

'Like a fairground ride,' he muttered.

He'd got maybe two miles in when he touched his foot to the brake.

'This OK?'

A fatman grunt. Oscar cut the engine and switched off the radio. They sat there quietly, the three of them, in the dense and liquid silence. Night-time, in the forest. Henry touched his groin. She's mine, he thought. She belongs to me. A sudden, wistful sigh, for the moment had almost come. It was almost there. They were almost in it.

'Dip the lights,' he said softly, 'and open the boot.'

He climbed outside, pulling the girl behind him, the fags still clutched in her thumb-tied hands. The air was damp on his face, moist with spores and country things. Oscar went round to the back and unlocked the petrol cap. He flicked on a torch and peered inside. Henry shook his head.

'Not now, OK? You can do that after.'

He held her by the arm and lifted up the boot.

'Got a job for you, first.'

The boy shone his torch inside.

'With the spade, you mean?'

'I want a nice little hole.'

'I fucking hate digging.'

'You swearing, son?'

Oscar hefted the spade. He flung the girl a poisonous glance.

'I reckon *she* should.'

'You retarded, Oswald?'

'I'm only suggesting.'

The boy shrugged his shoulders, slouched morosely off. There was the briefest intermission, then the sound of reluctant shovelling in loose, unfrozen earth. Henry drew her close, bent towards her ear.

'And then there were two . . .'

He pulled open his tie and loosened the belt, listening to Oscar grunting in the dark. Switching hands, still holding her tight, he eased off the jacket, let it fall to the ground. Shame about the suit, he thought, but a bloke had to do what a bloke had to do. He watched her eyes as they locked on the holster, saw panic ripple through her face. I'm me, he thought, and I'm fucking great. He heard the young guy breaking sweat, and felt the slut-bitch start to quiver, and judged himself a happy man.

'Don't worry, sugar.'

Unzipping his trousers.

'Be over soon.'

He felt her trying to push him away. Still tied at the thumbs, like a supplicant.

'It's OK,' he soothed, 'I'm not gonna hurt you.'

And he smacked her face with the back of his hand. Sounds loud in the forest, when a man like him slaps a girl like her.

'Got to pay for it, sweetheart. It's time to collect.'

The warmth in the groin. The chill in the air. The seductive scrape of a metal spade. Oh joy, he thought. Oh decadence.

And what of her, the heart and soul, the beating core, the reason they were there? What hope was in her battered head, what thoughts conspired to flood her brain, what sweet illusions of another life? You could have split her skull and poked inside, but there's nothing there. There's just a vacant space, just an emptiness, because she's waiting for oblivion. She shivered in the frozen air. Not long, she realized. Be over soon. Oh mother come and help me now.

He pushed her back against the car. Untied her thumbs.

'Over the bonnet, if you wouldn't mind.'

The relentless scrape of a metal spade. She was shaking, now, she was trembling bad. She shoved a ciggy in her mouth. He plucked it out and tossed it away.

'Come on, gorgeous. You know it makes sense.'

'Just one . . .' she whispered.

'We're wasting time.'

'Just let me . . .'

'No.'

'Just one last fag.'

'You begging?'

'No, I—'

'You begging?'

'Yes.'

He turned his head. The boy had stopped digging and was quietly watching.

'Should we let her, son?'

'Just a puff, boss, shall we? I mean we don't want to spoil her.'

Henry nodded.

'Mustn't do that.'

So he let her fumble with the ciggies. Watched her move about a yard away. She had purple shadows beneath her eyes. Half-dead anyway, he told himself.

'You got to answer, sugar, for all your crimes.'

'I know I do.'

She slid a fag between her lips and struck a match. Sucked

the filth inside her lungs. Not long now, she told herself. Be over soon.

'But first we have to answer for Joey, see?'

She took a breath of forest air. All finished, she realized. God save me now. One final drag on the nicotine, and she tossed the flame into the petrol tank. There was an endless moment of infinite horror, and the sudden bliss of nothingness.

Then rest in peace. Then fuck them all. Then Donna bitch in paradise.